PAY DIRT

Jim Payne, Sheriff of Cedar Springs, was only delivering his ma's letter to his estranged brother, Michael. Golden Gulch was a dangerous Californian boomtown, in the grip of the ruthless conman Coleridge Craven and his henchman, Kid Cassidy. Jim delivers the letter, but it seems Golden Gulch doesn't want him to go. He must face an old family feud, a miners' revolt and the murderous intentions of Craven and the Kid, if he wants to leave Golden Gulch alive . . .

Books by Lee Walker
in the Linford Western Library:

GUN LAW

LEE WALKER

PAY DIRT

Complete and Unabridged

LINFORD
Leicester

First published in Great Britain in 2012 by
Robert Hale Limited
London

First Linford Edition
published 2013
by arrangement with
Robert Hale Limited
London

A catalogue record for this book is available
from the British Library.

ISBN 978–1–4448–1565–8

Published by
F. A. Thorpe (Publishing)
Anstey, Leicestershire

Set by Words & Graphics Ltd.
Anstey, Leicestershire
Printed and bound in Great Britain by
T. J. International Ltd., Padstow, Cornwall

This book is printed on acid-free paper

For Dad

Prologue

The barn is on fire!

Thick smoke hangs like an angry cloud above the roof as yellow flames lick out of the hayloft door, bright against the twilight sky. The two mares are screaming in their stalls, kicking furiously at the back walls. Little Jimmy Payne drops the bucket of corn he was taking to the chickens and runs back across the yard.

The dogs bark furiously as he hauls at the giant barn door but it doesn't move an inch. He yells for help even though he knows his ma is with the neighbours half a mile down the track and his older brother Michael is fishing in the creek. The last time Jimmy saw Pa, he was working in the barn.

He hauls at the door again. This time it opens just wide enough for him to slide through as a wave of heat rushes over him. He's only ten and he's the most scared he's ever been in his life but he knows he's got to go in. He covers his mouth with his arm and peers through the smoke. In the middle of the barn, Pa is lying under the plough, his leg pinned fast. Beside him, a kerosene lamp is lying on its side in a circle of scorched hay. How many times had his Pa warned them to be careful of knocking over that lamp?

'Get back, Jimmy, get back, son!' Pa shouts as he sees him coming through the door.

Pa's breeches are starting to smoulder as the fire slowly closes in. All around, flames lick up the walls, around the windows and across the roof as though deliberately trying to cut off every means of escape.

Suddenly the boy realizes that if he doesn't do something, his pa is going to die; and he's going to die with him. He runs across the barn floor, flames snatching at his legs. He grabs the side of the plough with both hands and even though the metal burns into his palms like a branding iron and he starts to sob with the pain, he doesn't let go.

Embers are floating through the smoke and he feels the heat scorching his lungs. His eyes are streaming as he hauls with all his might against the plough, cursing himself for being so small and weak but the plough will not move. If only Michael was here . . . He looks around trying to find something he can use as a lever but it seems there is not a piece of wood that is not ablaze.

'Get out, son, get outta here!'

'No, Pa. No!' he shouts as he pours all his fury into the plough and tries to block out the sound of his pa's tortured coughs and the horses' screams.

And then he hears voices outside. Ma; and Michael too!

'Jimmy? Jimmy? Sweet Jesus, son, are you in there?'

'Pa? Where are you, Pa?' shouts Michael.

The boy looks down. Pa frantically

waves him away then lays his head down on the straw, exhausted by the heat and the smoke. High above, rafters begin to creak and the centre beam starts to sag and bend as though it too, can't take any more.

The horses are silent now.

Jimmy closes his eyes, runs to the door, trips and falls but manages to crawl outside just as the roof collapses and crashes on to the place where the plough had stood. Hands grab him and haul him into the night.

Then he is lying on the ground filling his lungs with sweet, cold air. His mother sobs as she rocks him in her arms and strokes his hair. She keeps saying something about his hands over and over again but he can't feel a thing. As he looks up into the clear night sky he thinks the stars look just like burning embers.

He turns to find his brother staring at him as though he hates him.

'Where's Pa . . . ?' is all Michael says.

1

Jim Payne stepped on to the rickety boardwalk and looked back at the stretch of wagon-ploughed mud he'd just crossed. He glanced down at his caked boots and spurs and quietly cursed.

It seemed to him that it was way too early to call the river of wet clay that split Golden Gulch Main Street but that's what the local miners had named it in their rush to build themselves a town.

Along each side of the chewed up thoroughfare, buildings were going up almost as fast as the canvas tents they were replacing. The air was heavy with a sickly blend of whip-sawn wood and whitewash. Work started at sunrise and didn't stop until last light every day of the week except Sundays. The oldest building had stood for no more than three months, but already saloons and stores were being extended with new storeys and false fronts. Their roofs and walls were covered in a forest of hand-painted signs offering everything a newly arrived prospector might need, as well as quite a few things he'd never considered. From coffee to coffins, anything could be had in Golden Gulch for a price.

Main Street was jammed with rigs and buckboards trying to plough through the water-filled potholes and high-sided ruts. Grey mud clung to wheels like thick glue. Drivers vented their anger on wallowing horses and mules but brutal whippings made no difference to their painfully slow progress.

Jim moved under the awning of a general store. He reached inside his dustcoat with a gloved hand, pulled out a thin cigar and slid it between his lips. He reached inside again, brought out a lucifer and with one deft stroke, scratched it down the nearest doorframe. As he held it to the cheroot, the stuttering flame lit the shadow below his battered Stetson.

His face was narrow and lean, bordering on handsome even with a week's worth of dark stubble around his strong jaw and lips. Although just in his thirties, his skin was weathered bronze and an uneven fringe of greying hair hung below the edge of the hat. The small flame made his eyes glow like slices of cold, blue ice. Then it guttered and his face was hidden in shadow once more.

He drew deeply and let a cloud of blue smoke escape through his nostrils as he studied the hordes of miners that passed.

Since the first gold nugget had been found in the sluice at Sutter's Mill just eight months ago, thousands had been lured to the American River, swelling the mining boomtowns that sprang up almost overnight. Now they were a giant rag-tag army in their uniforms of battered hats, dirt-caked dungarees and worn canvas shirts. Every man carried a pick, shovel or both. They spoke coarsely to each other through thick, shaggy beards, in tongues and accents the stranger didn't always recognize and what little of their faces could be seen was blackened by charcoal campfires.

In his mud-covered clothes, Jim looked like any other Argonaut ready to take his chance at the diggings, so no one paid him any heed as he scoured the river of faces. He had left his home in Cedar Falls, Iowa, three months ago and now that he had nearly come to the end of his mission all he wanted was to leave as quick and as quietly as he could, once he'd found the man he was looking for.

Across the street, standing on a broken packing crate half-sunk in the mud, a white-haired preacher in a dirt-spattered suit held a Bible high in the air. Jim listened as he appealed to his flock with hellish threats and heavenly promises. His strident voice rose above the street noise.

8

' . . . *and he that overcometh shall inherit all things but the fearful and the unbelieving and the abominable and murderers and whoremongers and sorcerers and idolaters and all liars shall have their part in the lake which burneth with fire and brimstone . . . '*

When the preacher turned, Jim saw that his eyes were blind discs of white.

He let his cigar drop to the boardwalk where he ground it with his boot. He pulled back his long coat. A well-oiled, low-slung holster was tied firmly against his left thigh. Within it nestled a pristine Colt Dragoon and, as he curled his fingers around its ivory handle, its smooth contours gave him comfort.

It was time to find the man he'd come to Golden Gulch for, but he wasn't sure where to start. Going around a place like this asking after a man was one sure-fire way of getting yourself noticed or killed; neither of which he intended to do.

His horse was being fed and watered

at the livery stable but now his own belly reminded him it hadn't had a hot meal for weeks. Once he'd got himself some grub, a bath and a bunk, he would think about how he was going to go about tracking down the man he wanted.

He looked down at his boots and cursed again. Leaning against the entrance to the store he kicked his heels against the doorjamb, trying to loosen the wad of mud that was starting to harden in the Californian sun.

Then he heard voices: angry voices. He listened to them arguing for a few moments, knowing it was none of his business. His first instinct was to investigate. His second was to walk away.

He gave in to the first.

2

The stranger peered into the store window that had 'CRAVEN MER-CANTILE' etched across it in large gold letters. Through carefully stacked pyramids of tins he watched an old prospector waving coffee in the face of a flustered clerk who stood behind a large wooden counter.

'I ain't paying this for a tin of Arbuckle's. This is downright daylight robbery!' the digger shouted.

'Sir, that's the price I gotta charge and — '

'We're slaving our backsides off standing knee high in that freezin' river all day gettin' mighty lean pickings o' pay dirt and that money grubbing boss o' yourn is taking what little we got right out of our back pockets.'

'I don't make the prices, sir, I only sell 'em at what I'm told.'

'Well, I'm tellin' you, sonny, me and these fellas have had about enough of this and we ain't prepared to go on fillin' the pockets o' your boss!'

A small crowd of miners had gathered around him, yelling and nodding their heads in agreement. The store clerk buckled under the noisy onslaught and backed away, fearing these men would come over the counter for him.

'Honestly fellas, I ain't — '

'Well you best go get your boss and tell 'im he'd better do something or — '

'Why don't you tell him yourself?' came a voice near the entrance to the store.

The miners fell silent as they turned to the speaker. The man was dressed in a black frock-coat and pants with a white shirt and thin black tie. He was tall and straight-backed with a head of thick black hair that fell at the back to his starched white collar. He sported a full black moustache and although he looked no more than thirty he spoke with the authority of someone much older; someone used to giving orders and having them obeyed without question. The clerk turned a sickly shade of pale as the man walked slowly towards the counter.

'What seems to be the problem here, Jamieson?'

'I'm sorry, Mr Craven, sir, but these here gentlemen ain't happy with some of our prices and — '

The miner banged the flat of his hand on the counter.

'Ain't happy? I'll say I ain't happy! Look here, Craven, seems your prices are going up quicker than a raccoon up a tree!'

Coleridge Craven stared at him. When he eventually spoke, it was in slow, measured tones.

'Well I'm sure sorry to hear that, mister, but if you ain't happy I guess you can go get your vittles from someplace else.'

The miner banged the counter again.

'Dammit, boy! You know we can't!

There ain't no other supplier 'less you want a two day ride to Sacramento, and you know we can't leave our diggin's lest some no-good claim-jumpin' sonofabitch moves in . . .'

Craven nodded thoughtfully, stroking his thick moustache with a thumb and forefinger.

'OK Let's see if I got this straight. You got everything you need right here under your nose, in buildings I put up, served by people I pay. You got all the saloons, eating-places and soiled doves you can use but that still ain't enough. Now you don't want to pay for 'em?'

'I never said I didn't . . .'

Craven held up his hand. The argument was over.

'I know what you said and you know what, mister? I think I've heard just about enough outta you. If you ain't buying, plenty others are and you're just gettin' in their way. So either pay for what you want or get the hell outta my store.'

The old miner's eyes narrowed.

'What if I told you I ain't got that sort of cash on me right now?'

'Then you can open an account. That's another service I provide. Jamieson here'll be glad to open one for you right now.'

'I've heard 'bout your tabs,' the old miner growled. 'You rack up interest on 'em so high some of these boys are handin' over all the pay dirt they find and they still owe you. I've heard of men goin' home owin' you more'n they ever earned.'

Craven pulled himself up to his full height and stuck his thumbs into his waistcoat pockets.

'Seems I just can't do nothin' right for you, can I? I think it's about time you were leavin'.'

'Now jist you wait a darned minute, boy . . .'

But Craven was already talking to the clerk. 'Go and get some of the boys to help this man outta my store, will you, Jamieson?'

The forty-niner suddenly leaned

forward and grabbed Craven's arm. 'You listen to me, Craven. You may think you own this whole damned town but one of these days you're gonna run up against some mean sonofabitch and you won't have your bunch of thugs behind ya. You mark my words, mister, your time'll come.'

Craven stared at the crushed sleeve of his freshly pressed coat. 'Get your filthy hands offa me,' he snarled.

'I ain't finished with ya!'

'But I'm finished with you . . . '

Without warning, Craven's right fist landed on the bridge of the miner's nose, breaking the cartilage with a sickening snap. As he fell back against the counter, a torrent of blood stained his unkempt moustache and beard. The next vicious punch bared his left cheekbone.

No one dared to intervene.

The old miner was out cold, sprawled across a pile of open sacks of corn, but Craven was now a man possessed of a fury beyond restraint or control.

Relentless, punishing blows rained down on the unfortunate miner who had dared commit the cardinal sin of questioning Craven's authority.

Craven raised his fist for yet another brutal blow, then stopped. His balled fist hung in mid-air as he heard the unmistakable cold metallic click of the hammer of a Colt Dragoon being firmly cocked and felt a small cold circle of steel shoved into the back of his neck.

'I think he's had enough, don't you?' said a quiet voice behind him.

Breathing heavily, Craven slowly straightened and brought his arms to his sides. His victim slid down the bags of corn and slumped to the floor like a child's discarded rag doll.

'Keep your hands where I can see 'em. Turn around real slow.'

Craven did as he was told and found the barrel of a rock-steady Dragoon aimed directly between his eyes.

'Get a doc, somebody!' said the gunman without taking his eyes from Craven.

The onlookers stood like dumb cattle for a few seconds, then four of them grabbed an arm or a leg and roughly heaved the unconscious miner out of the store.

As they went Craven took his time looking the stranger over. He was unimpressed with his trail-battered clothes and reckoned a bath and a shave wouldn't be wasted on him, but there was no mistaking the cool stare of his blue eyes looking down the gun barrel that told Craven this man, if provoked, would not hesitate to kill him.

'What's your name, stranger?' asked Craven quietly.

'No need for you to know.'

'Oh, I think there is,' Craven smiled. 'You don't want to end your days in an unmarked grave, do you? Least I can do is put your fool name on it.'

The stranger leaned forward and felt inside Craven's jacket. He lifted out a steel-bladed throwing knife from a sheath slung under his arm. 'That's mighty brave talk from a man in your position.'

'You're new to Golden Gulch,' said Craven as he brought his arms down and straightened the sleeves of his frock coat. It was a statement, not a question.

'Just in.'

'Figured that. So you won't know the golden rule round these parts?'

'And what that might be?'

'That the man with the gold makes the rules; and the man with the gold is me.'

'Is that a fact?'

'That's a fact. I don't take kindly to bums like you meddlin' in my affairs.'

'Your affairs ain't above the law.'

'I know my rights.'

'Your rights don't include beatin' a man to death.'

Craven smiled. 'If you were staying you'd get to learn I'm about all the law Golden Gulch has got. But you won't be staying,' he added.

'I like to decide for myself where and when I go.'

Craven watched him for a moment, then smiled again.

'I'll tell you what, mister. I'm gonna do you a favour. I'm gonna give you five minutes to get your sorry hide outta my sight. Don't waste it. You don't get a second chance.'

'I sure appreciate your kind offer but I plan to stay on in Golden Gulch a little while longer'n that. Got some business of my own to attend to.'

'I'm giving you fair warning,' said Craven, glaring at this man who kept daring to defy him. 'You cross my path again and you won't live to see tomorrow.'

The stranger touched the edge of his Stetson and smiled. 'Thanks for the warning. I'll take my chances.'

He started to back towards the door. When he reached it he dropped the Dragoon back into his holster.

'Just for the record, my name's Payne. Jim Payne.'

'I won't forget it,' snarled Craven as he watched the stranger disappear into the sunlight. He spat noisily on to the dusty wooden floor, then turned to the clerk.

'Go get the Kid. Tell him to find out what business this Payne fella has in Golden Gulch.'

Jamieson hurriedly untied his white apron and threw it on the bar. He was nearly out of the door with his jacket half-on when Craven called him again.

'And Jamieson?'

'Yes, Mr Craven?'

'Tell the Kid I don't want him dead 'til I say so.'

'Yes, Mr Craven, sir,' gulped Jamieson before scurrying out through the door.

3

Jim Payne crossed the boardwalk and stepped down into the mud-filled street again. As he passed a horse trough, he lightly tossed Craven's knife into the dirty water where it disappeared with a quiet splash.

Word of the stand-off had spread quickly and a small crowd had gathered outside the store. Payne could feel their stares as he crossed the street but he kept his eyes fixed forward, resisting the urge to look back over his shoulder. In situations like this he knew that as long as he kept his hand away from his gun he was as safe as he could be. Even in a lawless place like Golden Gulch no one took kindly to a man getting gunned down from the back.

He stepped up on to the opposite boardwalk and blended in with the stream of miners making their way along it. As he walked, he cursed himself for running up against someone like Craven so soon. Every bone in his body had told him to mind his own business. So why hadn't he?

As if answering his own question, Payne slipped his hand into his coat pocket and felt the familiar five-point outline of his sheriff's badge. All it did was remind him that although he might be a well-respected lawman back in Cedar Falls, here in Golden Gulch, he was just another nobody. Here, the badge meant nothing: no authority, no jurisdiction and no protection.

He'd been lucky to walk away from his run-in with Craven and he knew that if he wanted to get out of this town alive he was going to have to turn a blind eye to the next piece of trouble that came knocking. That didn't come easy. After nearly four years of trying to fulfil the obligations that came with wearing that badge, doing the right thing had become a kind of a habit. Here, doing the right thing was likely to get you killed.

Besides, he had a job to do . . . and it was nothing to do with protecting the citizens of Golden Gulch.

For about the hundredth time since he'd left Cedar Falls he put his hand into his shirt pocket and pulled out a letter. His ma's small spidery handwriting stretched across the hand-made envelope, sealed with a splash of wax. It was addressed to 'My Darling Son, Michael G. Payne.'

This was the piece of paper that had brought him all the way from Cedar Falls and he wouldn't rest until he'd delivered it into his brother's hand, just like he'd promised Ma. He just hadn't worked out exactly how he was going to do that.

Suddenly, Payne felt exhausted. Weeks of constant travelling on just a few hours sleep had finally caught up with him and he knew he couldn't risk being tired. Tired men were slow, and slow, in a place like Golden Gulch, could mean dead.

Right now he needed a place to eat and somewhere to clean up and rest for a while. Then he would deal with his brother. Payne was deep in thought as he stepped from the sidewalk to cross an alleyway and by the time he saw the sudden flash of silver out of the corner of his eye, it was too late.

A cold edge of steel pressed against his throat so hard he was sure it had drawn blood. His left wrist was grabbed in a vicelike grip as he instinctively went for his gun. As he was dragged into the narrow alleyway, a whiskey-filled breath whispered in his ear.

'Nice 'n easy, mister. Jist keep quiet and you won't get hurt.'

'Who are you? Whadya want?' gasped Payne, straining his neck to keep his throat away from the deadly blade.

'That don't matter fer now, mister. Jist keep still and listen up.'

Payne knew to do as he was told.

'Heard you tried to take on Coleridge Craven. That right?'

Payne nodded and heard a chuckle

bubble in the man's chest.

'Ain't many men done that and lived to tell the tale. Come to think on it, I don't recall a single one.'

Payne didn't reply. This was no ordinary bushwhacking. If it was his money or horse or gun he was after, it would have been over by now, the road agent far away, leaving Payne dead or dying in a pool of his own blood. This fella wanted to talk.

'So what brings a man like you to Golden Gulch, mister?'

'Same as everybody else.'

'Naw, naw,' laughed the knifeman, 'you ain't here to dig.' He yanked the knife closer to Payne's throat and he let out a grunt. 'Hurts, don't it? Now if you don't want me to gut you like a catfish, I propose you start tellin' me the truth. What's your business? You gotta score to settle with Craven? Huh?'

Payne shook his head as best he could. 'I never set eyes on him before I rode in today.'

'C'mon, stranger. What sort of a fool d'you take me for? You ride in here and just decide to save the hide of some old digger? You pull a gun on the man that owns half this town and you ain't gotta beef with him?'

'I ain't got a beef with no one. I told you. I'm here for the gold.'

'So how come you didn't plug him when you had the chance?'

'I ain't a killer.'

'Well, you made one helluva mistake, cos he is. I wouldn't be making plans on doing nothing important tomorrow if I were you.'

'If he wants me out of the way so bad, I'll go.'

'Ain't as easy as that.'

'Look, what is it you want from me?'

'First, I wanna know what your business is in Golden Gulch.'

'It's a long story.'

'I got time.'

Payne swallowed and his Adam's apple scraped against the knife.

'Trouble is, hard to think straight with your knife shaving my chin. What say you back up a bit and cut me some slack?'

There was a brief silence. 'Don't try nothin' funny,' said the knifeman eventually.

Payne felt the man's grip relax a fraction. It was all he needed. As fast as a rattlesnake, he kicked back viciously and felt his spur sink into the man's shin, through fabric and flesh, and then grate sickeningly against bone.

The bushwhacker sprang back, howling with pain, grabbing his badly gashed leg with both hands. Payne spun around and rammed his open palm under the man's jaw with all his strength. The head jerked back as though kicked by a small horse and smashed against the side of the wooden building.

As the bushwhacker slipped into unconsciousness, his long, sleek Bowie knife fell to the ground. Before it touched earth, Payne had swung his

Dragoon out of its holster and jammed the barrel into the man's neck. For the first time, Payne got a look at his attacker.

4

Coleridge Craven didn't know how long he had paced up and down his rug-covered office above the Blood & Sweat saloon. He glanced frequently at the French grandfather clock standing in the corner and decided it was running slow, but when he checked it against his silver pocket watch they both had the same time. The fact was, Craven was waiting and he was just no good at it. He lit himself a large cigar but it did little to soothe his agitation.

In frustration, he swung open the office door and strode out into the corridor, past the dozen bedrooms that could be rented by the hour. He stopped at the top of the flight of stairs which lead to the busy saloon below. It was a good vantage point and Craven often stood there surveying his business. From here he could see what was going on and his staff and customers could see him.

He looked over the side of the rail to the large roulette table which he had shipped in all the way from a casino in Washington. He thought the two-foot golden spike in the centre of the wheel was a nice touch; a fitting reminder of the source of his wealth.

Normally, he would have watched the spinning numbers for a while, knowing they were stacked in his favour, and judging by the number of men round the table the takings he was likely to rake in.

But today he couldn't concentrate. Impatiently, he tapped his fingers on the rail, then angrily turned and strode back into his office, slamming the door behind him. He threw himself into the chair behind his wide oak desk and puffed on the cigar clenched between his teeth.

The ornate grandfather clock told him another nine minutes had passed before he heard steps coming along the corridor.

'Where the hell have you been?' growled Craven as Kid Cassidy came into the room.

The young man was tall and slim. His dark-skinned face was handsome with a strong jaw, full lips and high cheekbones that hinted at Indian somewhere in his bloodline. His eyes, deep set and narrow, held real menace. From his Stetson to his hand carved boots, his black clothes were expensive and sat on him well. As he came into the room, he brushed trail dust from his sleeve.

'I was upriver checking on the boys like you told me to. Making sure all your gold got in the river and stayed outta their pockets.'

'Did Jamieson speak to you?'

'Just got back. Ain't seen nobody.'

Craven pushed out of his chair and went to the window overlooking Main Street. He held back the drape with the back of his hand and puffed on his cigar angrily.

'You're meant to be around when I

need you, Kid. If there's any trouble you should be here. Ain't that why you're on the payroll? Well? Ain't it?' Craven was almost shouting.

The Kid put both hands up in mock surrender.

'Whoa, whoa, Cole! What the hell's the matter? What's happened?'

Cole swung round angrily and jabbed his cigar at the young man.

'I'll tell you what's happened. Some bum came into the store and pulled a gun on me. Took my knife off me then made off. In my own store. In my own town, dammit!' Craven banged the table in frustration.

'Who was this guy?'

'Never set eyes on him before.'

'You sure?'

'Oh, I'm sure all right. I would've remembered. There was something about him.'

'How d'ya mean?'

Craven returned to the window and gazed out.

'He wasn't the usual mug we get

through here. He was quiet but . . . I don't know . . . he wasn't scared to kill and . . . '

'And what, Cole?'

' . . . he didn't look scared to die, either.'

'D'you get his name?'

'Payne. Jim Payne.'

'What was he like?'

'Tall. Scrawny. Looked like he'd been travelling for weeks. A southpaw. Wears a tan glove on his right hand.'

'What was he packin'?'

'Dragoon.'

'Say what he was here for?'

Craven shook his head. 'That was the thing. Said he had his own business to attend to. One thing's for sure, he's not here for gold. He's looking for something else.'

'Or somebody?'

'Maybe.'

Craven sat down again.

'He's trouble. I sense it. I don't want him sniffing around the river. We don't need this Payne fella pokin' his nose in where it don't belong.'

'Sure thing. I'll ask around. I'll find him.'

The Kid turned to leave.

'Kid?'

'Yeah?'

'First, go to the café. Get Edith.'

'Sure thing, boss. Anything else?'

Craven took a long slow draw on his cigar and watched the smoke rise up leisurely to the ceiling.

'Yeah. When you find Payne, keep him alive . . . for now.'

'Sure. For now . . . ' The Kid smiled as he left the office.

5

Jim stared at the lined and cracked face of the old miner, barely visible behind a mass of matted grey hair and whiskers as he pressed the gun into his neck and shook him until he came to.

'Can you hear me, old-timer?'

The miner nodded groggily as he came to.

'Now, before I blow your damn fool head off, you'd better start tellin' me who you are and what the hell you think you're doing!'

The miner blinked and shook his head. Tobacco-stained saliva rolled down his beard as he began to stammer.

'Murphy. The name's Murphy. Seamus Murphy, but everybody round here calls me Dusty.'

'Keep talkin', Dusty.'

'I didn't mean no harm. Honest, son.

Jest wanted to talk . . . '

'So talk,' snarled Jim, ramming the gun harder into Murphy's fleshy neck.

'I was at the store earlier. I saw how you handled Craven. I thought maybe you could help. Look, mister, I ain't even got a gun . . . '

Jim stared into the old-timer's rheumy eyes.

'Why didn't you just come up and talk 'stead of sneakin' up on me like a coyote?'

'Are you crazy? I couldn't be seen with ya! Craven's got spies everywhere. If the Kid found out I'd been talkin' to ya — '

'Who's the Kid?'

'Say, you *are* new to town. Kid Cassidy, of course. Craven uses him to keep the peace around here. Heads up his own gang of killers. He'll know about you by now but you wanna stay out of his way.'

Jim stared at the old man. He wasn't happy with the way he'd been jumped but he could tell Dusty Murphy was telling the truth and, disarmed, seemed pretty harmless.

'Look mister, could you put the gun down? I swear on my life, I didn't mean nothin'.'

Slowly, Jim let his grip loosen on the miner's shirt and took a few paces back, keeping the Dragoon trained on him. Dusty Murphy breathed a sigh of relief but didn't try and get up. He stayed in the mud with his back against the lapboard building, rubbing his bleeding shin.

'So what d'ya want from me?'

Dusty looked up. 'Coleridge Craven.'

'What about him?'

'You saw what he's like. He's gotta noose around this town and it's gettin' tighter every day. He's bleedin' us dry.'

'Last time I checked, weren't no law 'gainst a man making money. It's a free country.'

'Hell, no! 'Course there ain't!' Dusty coughed up a large ball of phlegm and spat on the ground. 'Ain't that the reason we're all here? Got no gripe with that. If them crazy bastards are mad enough to pay what he asks, ain't my concern.'

'So what *is* your gripe?'

The old miner looked from one end of the alley to the other as though someone might be listening. Then he leaned forward.

'He's saltin' the river,' he whispered.

'He's what?'

'Saltin' the river,' the old man repeated. 'He's dumping gold dust into it.'

Jim laughed. 'You're crazy. Why would he do that?'

''Cause there ain't no gold left!'

Jim said nothing as he watched the old man struggle to his feet, trying to put weight on his injured leg. 'Why would a businessman like Craven dump all of his profits in the river?'

Dusty spat again and tapped the side of his head with a dirty finger. 'Say, boy, you're mighty fast with that gun but you ain't so quick up here, are you?'

Jim smiled at the insult and let it

pass. 'So tell me.'

'It's real simple. Once those Argo-nauts stop finding gold, they'll go. Craven'll be bust and Golden Gulch'll be a ghost town before you can say 'pay dirt' but if they keep findin' gold they stay and Craven can keep chargin' what he likes. Not only that, word of gold spreads like wildfire. All Craven has to do is put some of his profits back into the river just to keep the gold fever on the boil. For every greenhorn that gives up another ten are just linin' up to take his place, just dyin' to give Craven top dollar for bad food and lousy booze.'

'How do you know all this?'

'I know a river that's been cleaned out of gold when I see it. These greenhorns find placers . . . '

Jim looked quizzical.

' . . . deposits of gold where they shouldn't be. It ain't natural, I'm tellin' you. And that's because Mother Nature didn't put 'em there, Craven's men did! But those fellas are so blinded by gold fever they don't care where they find it as long as it keeps comin'. I've been pannin' gold for longer than I care to remember and I know what he's doin'. I jist can't prove it and even if I could, I wouldn't stand a chance against Craven and his men!'

Jim rubbed his chin thoughtfully. 'Let's say you're right. Let's say Craven is a crook. What's it got to do with me?'

Dusty closed one eye and looked the young man up and down.

'Mister, in six months or so I've been here, you're the only man I've seen that's dared to stand up to Craven and lived to tell the tale. With you at our head the rest would rally round and . . . '

'Whoa, whoa, old man,' said Jim, 'you got me all figured wrong. I ain't no hired gun. Don't go getting confused with what you saw today. Sure, I ain't gonna stand by and watch him kill a man, but the way he runs his business ain't my business. You wanna start a revolution, best get someone else.'

'We had someone else. A couple of

41

months back. A young fella name of Jack Winsome. He knew what Craven was up to and wasn't scared of speakin' his mind.'

'What happened to him?'

'Got gunned down in the street not far from here.'

'And you think Craven was behind it?'

'Bet a gold mine on it!'

Jim shook his head. 'This still ain't none of my business.'

Dusty grabbed his arm. 'If it's money you're after, we can pay you. We got gold . . . '

'I ain't interested in gold!'

Dusty started sniggering. His shoulders shook and then he started laughing right out loud, slapping his thigh until tears filled his eyes.

'You ain't interested in gold?' he managed to say. 'You must be the only man in a five hundred mile circle who ain't! Ain't interested in gold? I never heard such a thing.'

Eventually he managed to pull

himself together. 'Well, if it ain't gold that's brought you to Golden Gulch, what has?'

Jim stared at the old-timer. Perhaps he could help. 'I'm looking for my brother. Name of Michael Payne. Came down this way a few months back.'

'He get the gold fever?'

'Seems like it.'

'Makes a man crazy. What's he like?'

'A lot like me. Same height. Same build. Bit older but when we were kids lots of folks mistook us for twins.'

'Got business with him?'

'Family business. Got a letter to deliver. As soon as I put it in his hand I get to go home.'

Dusty rubbed his beard and his eyes narrowed.

'I gits the feelin' there's some bad blood between ya. Am I right?'

Jim slid the Dragoon back into the holster.

'Either you can help or you can't. I don't have time to stand around jawin' all day.'

'OK, OK! Don't go gettin' into a lather boy. I'll ask around. If he's here, I'll find him.'

'I'd appreciate that.'

Dusty Miller put out his hand and Jim shook it firmly. 'Now suppose you tell me where I can get some good chow.'

'Sure. Go up, end of the street, second shop on the right. A place called The Tuckered Out Café. Remember Jack, the fella that got murdered? His widow runs the place. Pretty gal, name of Edith Winsome. Best grub in town.'

'Thanks. If you get news of Michael, that's where I'll be.'

Jim lifted the old man's battered hat out of the mud and put it on his head.

'You'd better get a doc to take a look at that leg. Next time you want a word with me, don't go jumping out of alleyways.'

6

Jim found the Tuckered Out Café easily.

Even if he hadn't had directions, he would have tracked it down just from the smell of fresh baked apple pie wafting out of the doorway. He couldn't remember when he had last sat down to a hot meal and the home-cooking smell made his belly ache. As he walked through the white-painted doors he sniffed strong, hot coffee.

Instinctively, Jim quickly looked around to get a measure of the place. The café wasn't big. There was just about enough room for the dozen tables covered in red-checked table-cloths. It was basic but clean and the food must have tasted as good as it smelled because it was standing room only. There were three or four men to every table and they were mostly too busy clearing their tin plates even to talk.

A counter ran halfway down one wall and behind it was a large black range with two steaming coffee jugs and a couple of other pots on the go. Serving behind the counter was a harassed-looking woman whom Jim took to be Edith Winsome, the owner Dusty had mentioned.

He had to admit she was a handsome woman. She looked to be in her thirties and although still pretty, her tired face said all her times hadn't been easy. Her plain grey dress was covered with a stained white apron and Jim watched her closely as she pushed back a stray lock of blonde hair that kept coming loose and spilling down over her striking blue eyes.

Women were outnumbered a hundred to one at the diggings and he couldn't help but wonder what had brought a woman as pretty as Edith to a place like Golden Gulch. But whatever troubles she may have had, earning a

46

living seemed to be the least of them. A queue of miners stretched out in front of the counter. Jim fell in line and slowly shuffled forward with them.

A chalkboard advertised the day's menu. Pork stew, beans, bacon, bread and apple pie. As at the general store, Jim noted the prices weren't cheap but, unlike Craven's place, everybody seemed happy to pay. Out here on the American River where men toiled hard and lived rough a long way from their home comforts, anything that resembled a taste of good home cooking was literally worth its weight in gold. Eventually it was his turn to be served.

'What'll it be?' asked Edith. She didn't look up as she piled up dirty plates and mugs.

'Pork stew, beans and coffee, ma'am. That'll do for a start,' said Payne.

Edith started pulling together his meal. As she handed over the tin plate, she looked up and saw Jim for the first time. She hesitated.

'Something wrong, ma'am?' asked
Jim.

'No . . . no . . . it's just that . . . '
Edith started to say and then stopped.
'Don't matter,' she said slapping stew
on to a tin plate.

'New around here, ain't ya?' she
asked as she splashed coffee into a mug.

Jim nodded. 'Just arrived this morning.'

'Say, you're not that guy, are you?'

'What guy might that be?'

'The fella that pulled his gun on
Coleridge Craven.'

Jim looked over his shoulder. The
miner behind him shuffled back a step
or two.

'Word travels fast.'

'Sure does, mister — 'specially when
it's concerning some lunatic who's tired
of livin'!'

She banged the coffee pot down hard
on the range, spilling some on to the
hot plate where it fizzled angrily.

'I ain't tired of livin' just yet, ma'am,'
said Jim quietly.

'Well, if that's so, take a piece of advice from someone who's been around Golden Gulch a lot longer'n you. You eat this and then get on your horse and you skedaddle off back to wherever you came from. If you think for one minute Craven or the Kid is going to let you see nightfall, you're more of a fool than I took you for, and you don't look much like a fool to me.'

Edith angrily pushed back the blonde spiral of hair that had fallen over the side of her face again. Her cheeks were flushed and red and there was a fire in her eyes that made them sparkle. She banged the coffee mug on the counter.

'Anyways, I've said way enough already,' she said as she dried her hands fiercely on her apron, 'and that's another thing you need to know 'bout Golden Gulch, mister There's always someone ready to scuttle back to Craven or the Kid with news of what's going on. So you be careful who you talk to and what you say.'

Jim lifted his plate and mug. 'Thanks for the advice.'

'Sure thing. Advice is free. Grub's two dollars. Next!'

He placed two dollars on the counter and found an empty table at the back of the café where he could keep his back to the wall and watch the front door to see who came and went. As a bonus, his vantage point gave him a clear view of Edith Winsome as she worked. He threw his coat and hat on the chair beside him and started to clear his plate, every now and then looking up hoping to catch her eye, but she was kept busy serving the constant stream of hungry miners.

He made short work of his meal, cleaned his plate with a chunk of bread, then pushed back in his chair and lit a cheroot. As he sipped the strong coffee, it warmed his bones and began to make him feel so drowsy he could have put his head on the table and gone to sleep there and then. But he had things to do and, according to Dusty and Edith, it didn't sound like he had a whole lot of time to do them before Craven or the Kid caught up with him.

With a bit of luck, if Dusty could find Michael, he might be able to deliver the letter by this evening and he could get out of this town, where it was beginning to feel he'd already outstayed his welcome.

His thoughts were interrupted as Edith came out from behind the counter and started clearing tables.

'Hey, Tommy. I could sure use some help out here!' she called over her shoulder.

A blond-haired boy reluctantly came out from behind the counter. Payne reckoned he was about eleven and there was no mistaking he was his mother's son. He took the pile of plates from his ma and was turning to go back into the kitchen when the door crashed open. A young man swaggered in, dressed in black from head to toe.

Nobody had to tell Jim he'd just met Kid Cassidy.

7

The Kid's eyes lighted on Edith. 'Hey, sugar. What's cooking?' he said as he made his way over with a wide smile that showed two rows of straight white teeth.

'Specials are up on the board. Take your pick,' she said and brushed past him on the way back to the counter.

'Boss wants to see you,' he called after her.

'Tell him I'm busy.'

'Don't think he cares. Wants to see you now.'

Edith banged a pile of plates on the counter and pushed back her lock of hair.

'Look, Kid, can't you see I'm up to my neck here? I got plates piled high and plenty more mouths to feed. Can you tell Cole I'll get over to the Blood & Sweat just as soon as I can?'

She made to walk past him but the Kid blocked her way. The smile had drained from his face.

Watching from the back of the café, Jim brought the legs of his chair to the floor. Under the table, he slid his hand to the Dragoon and quietly pulled the hammer back.

'I don't think you heard me right,' the Kid said quietly. 'I ain't gonna argue with you no more'n I'd argue with my dog. When the boss says 'come' you come like the good little bitch you are — unless of course you want me and the boys to close down your little café permanent. Then you won't be too busy to do what the boss asks. Want me to do that?'

'No,' murmured Edith staring at the floor.

'Seems to me you're forgettin' the only reason you got this place is that you got Cole's protection. I think you should show a little bit more appreciation, don't you?'

Edith stared at the floor.

'Don't think I heard you right.'

'Yes . . . sir . . . ' said Edith. As she raised her head to look at the Kid, Jim saw a defiant flash of anger in her eyes.

'Well, that's a whole lot better. Let's go.'

The Kid grabbed Edith roughly by the arm and pulled her towards the door.

'You let my ma go!' shouted Tommy as he ran across the café and punched the young gunslinger in the small of the back. Kid Cassidy looked down at the boy as though he was an insect.

'Outta my way, boy, before you get hurt.'

The boy punched him again. The Kid swung the back of his hand across his chest and smacked the boy on the side of his face. Tommy flew back, landed heavily on a chair, then tumbled on to the floor.

'Tommy!' screamed Edith and made to go to him.

The Kid held her.

'He's fine. I just tapped him. Now

come on — I've wasted enough time on you and your runt!' snarled the Kid pulling Edith towards the door. She tried to resist but the Kid was strong and her shoes slipped across the floorboards. They didn't reach the door.

Jim stood with his arms folded in front of the door.

'You gotta real nice way with women and children, son,' he said.

'Who the hell are you callin' 'son', you piece of horseshit?' snarled the Kid, 'You best get outta my face, stranger, before I send you to hell.'

'Don't do this, mister. He'll kill you!' pleaded Edith, staring into Jim's eyes.

The Kid smiled broadly. 'You heard the lady. Now I ain't gonna tell you again. Get outta my way!'

'Let her go,' said Jim quietly.

The Kid looked the newcomer up and down for a few moments. He gauged his height to be that of his own, the battered clothes, the low slung Dragoon and the tan glove. He stared at the stranger's eyes and suddenly recognized what Craven had told him. It was unusual for the Kid to look into the eyes of another man and not see at least a flicker of fear. A smile of recognition spread across his face.

'Hey, wait a minute,' he said, 'you ain't the *hombre* who stood up to Cole Craven are you?'

Jim said nothing.

'Well, well. Good to run in to you. This kills two birds with one stone. I was going to be looking for you later on. Saves me a lot of trouble.'

'I don't know about that. I might be more trouble than you know how to handle.'

The Kid smiled broadly.

'You sure make a habit of meddlin' in other folks' business, don't you?'

'So far all I've seen of you and your boss's business is beatin' up kids, women and unarmed old men. So sure, I poke my nose in when I need to.'

The Kid felt a flare of anger in the pit of his stomach. It soared into his head and burned behind his eyes. He cursed

Craven's instructions to keep this bum alive.

'Nobody speaks to me like that.'

'I just did.'

'You wanna die?' the Kid almost screamed. 'Do you?'

Suddenly both men went for their guns. Before anyone knew what was happening the two gunmen had their weapons pointing at each other's foreheads, not two feet separating them. Neither man showed fear, both were equally capable of pulling the trigger.

'Stop it! Stop it!' screamed Edith as she put herself between them. She turned on Jim furiously.

'This is no business of yours. Who do you think you are — some kinda white knight? You wanna get us all killed? What is it with you men and your goddamn guns? I don't need you to fight my fights, mister. I can take care of myself!'

Tommy let out a low groan and stirred on the floor. Edith ran to his side.

'You all right, darlin'?'

'I'm fine, Ma.'

She flattened his hair and stroked his cheek where a livid bruise was already beginning to form.

'Will you be OK? I gotta go with the Kid for a little while. Can you take care of things 'til I get back?'

She turned to the two men.

'You can put your guns away now.'

Reluctantly, both men uncocked their guns and put them back in their holsters.

Edith walked over to the two men.

'C'mon Kid. You don't want to waste a bullet on him. Let's go. We've kept Cole waiting long enough.'

As Jim stood aside to let them pass, Kid Cassidy stopped.

'I gotta go, stranger, but I'll be back. I'm gonna enjoy puttin' a bullet through your thick skull and next time there won't be a woman you can hide behind.'

Jim watched silently as Edith and the Kid crossed the street and disappeared into the Blood & Sweat Saloon. He felt a fool. Twice now, he'd put his life on the line. For what? He made his way back to his table, put on his hat and hung his coat over his arm before checking again that the letter was safe.

He reckoned there was nothing worth fighting for in Golden Gulch but if he didn't stop acting like a sheriff, he was likely to get his head shot off for nothing. As he passed the boy he stopped.

'You OK, son?'

Tommy nodded.

'You did a brave thing there.'

The boy looked up at him and grinned. 'So did you.'

Jim was still smiling at the boy when the door of the café burst open. He swung round and drew his gun as diners ducked below the table.

'Hey! Hold your fire! It's me!' Dusty shouted, holding his hands up.

Jim cursed under his breath and put his gun away.

'I swear to God, Dusty, you're gonna

get yourself killed jumpin' up on me all the time.'

Dusty Murphy smiled broadly. 'You're in luck, stranger. I think I found your brother!'

8

Coleridge Craven was behind his desk, shuffling some papers, when Kid Cassidy and Edith came into his office. He didn't look up.

'What kept you both?'

'Bumped into your friend,' said the Kid.

Cole raised his eyes. 'You talk to Payne?'

'In a manner of speakin'.'

'I ain't in the mood for games, Kid. What happened?'

'Well, I went to the café like you told me to. Edith here wasn't too keen to come see you so I had to persuade her.'

'You hit my son, you . . . ' Edith began angrily.

Cole raised his hand. 'I'll deal with you in a minute, Edith. Please, sit down.'

Edith did as she was told. She could

tell Craven was in one of his foul moods.

'So what happened?' continued Craven.

'He tried to get in between me and Edith. We had words. Ended up pulling guns on each other. I was gonna plug him but I reckoned you wouldn't be too happy if I killed him seeing as you wanted to find out what he was doing here.'

'You reckoned right.'

'So, if it's all the same to you, as soon as I'm done here, I'm goin' back to find him and finish the job.' He glanced over at Edith. 'This time, there won't be no one to get in the way.'

Craven nodded.

'OK. Come back when you know anything.'

The Kid turned and, with a last glare at Edith, left the office.

The silence in the room was broken only by the muffled sounds of the saloon below and the slow heavy tick of the grandfather clock. Craven looked at Edith who stared at the floor.

'Well, well, well,' said Craven eventually as though addressing a child. 'What am I to do with you, Edith?'

He got up from behind his desk and sat beside her. Edith shifted uncomfortably along the leather sofa.

'Here we go again. I ask you to come over and see me; to see if you had reconsidered my offer, and then I go and find out you've been causing problems for me. Frankly, Edith, I'm disappointed. I expected more from my fiancée.'

'I am not your fiancée,' said Edith, her eyes flaring with anger.

'I know, I know. Not officially. Not yet. But I'm nothing if not persistent. I've asked you a couple of times now and you know I don't like 'no' for an answer. I'm not the kind of man who usually asks twice for what I want — hell, sometimes I don't even ask once — but I'll make an exception in your case. So, I'm asking you again. Will you marry me?'

Edith stared at the toes of her boots

that peeped out from beneath her dress.

'I can't,' she said quietly.

Craven's eyes narrowed. 'You can't or you won't?'

'Both.'

Craven rose and walked to the centre of the room, his thumbs hooked deep into the front pockets of his waistcoat.

'What's the problem, Edith? What more do I have to do? Ain't I good enough for you? I let you work your little café when I could close you down like that!' he said, snapping his fingers. 'I make sure nothin' happens to you. Ain't I looked after you and the boy like I promised I would after Jack had his accident?'

Edith jumped to her feet.

'His *accident*? Is that what you're *still* callin' it, Cole?'

'It was terrible what happened, but — '

'It was no accident. One of your men gunned my husband down like he was a dog in the street . . . '

'Not one of my men . . . '

' . . . just because he spoke out about the way things were going in Golden Gulch . . . '

' . . . he shouldn't've got involved . . . '

' . . . he never trusted you . . . '

' . . . he was a meddler in things that . . . '

' . . . *he knew you were a liar and a thief!*' screamed Edith.

She froze, frightened at her anger and the words she had often thought but never had the courage to say. Cole's back straightened as he watched Edith in front of him, her face flushed with anger, her breasts heaving, and he thought he had never seen her look so beautiful. She lifted a trembling hand to her lips as though to take the words back.

'Jack was a good man,' she said eventually, trying to control her quavering voice. 'He was a family man. He loved Tommy and me in a way you couldn't understand. We were happy 'til he heard about the gold getting pulled out of that river. He would still be alive if we hadn't come to Golden Gulch.'

'Jack didn't know how to mind his own business.'

'He was sure you were salting the river. Is it true, Cole? Are you? Is that why you had him killed?'

Craven turned away from her piercing stare.

'You have to look after yourself now, Edith. You and the boy. Don't go making the mistakes Jack did.'

Edith took a deep breath. 'I intend to. Listen to me, Cole. I need you to understand that I cannot now nor ever will be able to accept your offer of marriage. The only man I ever loved was cruelly taken from me and, I'm sorry to say, despite your protests, I think you were behind it. I don't think I can ever love again. Not you. Not anybody. And if that means I can no longer afford your 'protection' then so be it. I guess I'll have to take my chances. All I want to do is to be left in peace, work in the café and look after my son until I have enough money to get out of here. I curse the day I ever stepped foot in Golden Gulch.'

Craven spread his thick moustache with a thumb and forefinger.

'Well, well. Quite a speech. You've been bottlin' that up for a while.'

'I guess I have.'

'And I can't change your mind?'

'Never.'

Craven smiled. 'Never say never, my dear.'

There was an uncomfortable silence before Edith spoke.

'May I go now?'

'You're free to go.'

'Thank you, Cole.'

She gathered her skirts and crossed the room. As she opened the door, Craven called after her.

'Edith?'

'Yes?'

'You do know that if I can't have you, no other man will. You know that, don't you?'

'Goodbye, Cole.'

As Edith stepped into the hallway

and quietly closed the door behind her, her legs felt suddenly weak. She leaned back against the door to stop herself from falling. She fought to catch a breath as her heart pounded in her chest.

For months she had tried to play Craven's game of cat and mouse. There was no doubt that making him and other people think she was his girl was useful for a while but it was a dangerous game to play.

She knew it had been a big mistake to say those things to him, but now that she had she felt excited and elated. Maybe that newcomer taking a stand against Craven and Kid Cassidy had something to do with it. Hadn't he shown you could stand up against these men? That they were not invincible?

But she knew that, for Tommy's sake, she couldn't stay in Golden Gulch. Tonight, after dark, she and Tommy would leave. Before she did, she needed to speak to the stranger.

9

Jim followed Dusty along Main Street down towards the wide, muddy river. Not for the first time he wondered what kind of madness had taken over this place. It seemed to him that, despite its newness, everything in Golden Gulch was already battered and worn by the relentless grind that was the search for gold. Everybody he passed looked bone weary. It seemed the only bright thing about them was the greed that shone in their eyes.

'I think he's down there,' said Dusty, pointing towards a wide, sandy river-bank where scores of men were standing thigh deep in the murky river water. Some were shovelling spadefuls of dirt into a newfangled contraption they were calling a cradle but most were bent over in the shallows, hypnotically staring into their slowly spinning pans. Every now and again they stopped to stick their little finger into the gravel, pushing it around for the small flash of sunlight that would mean they had found gold. Payne had seen his share of desperate men; he'd just never seen so many in one place at one time.

'Is there *anybody* striking it rich here, Dusty?'

Dusty spat a large wad of evil-coloured tobacco into the sand.

'Couple of guys got nearly five thousand dollars apiece. 'Course, that was in the early days. It's like everything else. You gotta get in early. But I ain't ever seen prospectin' like this before. In the old days a man could spend a month in the mountains before you got a sniff of hide or hair of another soul. Now look at 'em,' he said, surveying the army of workers. 'These guys are just shiftin' gravel but that don't stop them from dawn to dusk. And when they're through for the day, they'll all need grub, gear, women and booze; all provided for by Mr Craven himself.'

Jim knew Dusty was convinced this was all one big scam concocted by Craven. Could he be right? Could one man fool so many, for so long? Did gold fever make them so blind to the truth?

He scoured the figures for a familiar face but they all looked the same in their dirty breeches held up with wide suspenders and wearing nothing on top but long johns and battered hats.

'I don't see my brother,' Jim muttered.

'C'mon,' said Dusty.

They made their way down the riverbank. Dusty approached a miner standing near the shallows, bent almost double. He was staring intently in his shallow pan, swirling it round in small tight circles, and every time he completed one revolution he let a little water slop over the side. He seemed lost to this world, oblivious to what was going on around him, hypnotized by

71

the small pile of dirt in the bottom of the pan.

It took him three attempts before Dusty got his attention.

''Scuse me, partner,' he said.

The panner reluctantly dragged his eyes away from the pile of gravel.

'What do you want?'

'Lookin' for someone.'

'What's his handle?'

'Payne. Michael Payne. Know him?'

The man straightened and stretched his back, groaning with the pain. 'Never heard of him,' he said and spat a wad of tobacco into the swirling river. Then he picked up his shovel, dropped another load of dirt into his pan and started swirling again.

'Sorry, Jim,' said Dusty,' I was told he was here for sure.'

Jim did his best to hide his disappointment. 'That's all right. You tried. Probably too much to ask to find him so quickly.'

The two men had just turned to go when another forty-niner standing close by called out. 'Couldn't help but hear you're lookin' for a man called Payne.'

The two men turned to see a tall man, painfully thin. His dark hair was long and his beard was bushy and unkempt, his clothes filthy and thread-bare. Jim couldn't help but notice his grazed and bleeding hands with broken nails.

'Know where I can find him?' asked Dusty.

'Who wants to know?' the man said.

Dusty pointed at Jim with his thumb. 'This fella here. Came all the way from Cedar Falls, Iowa. Got a letter for him.'

The miner rubbed his beard thought-fully. 'Might be able to help . . . '

'Can you take us to him?' said Dusty.

'I might . . . I might . . . what's it worth to you?'

Dusty turned to Jim. 'You got cash? Only way things happen around here.'

Jim peeled off two dollars from a tight roll and handed them to the miner who stuffed them into the pocket of his pants. Then he smiled broadly, showing a mouthful of rotten teeth.

'Hello, little brother,' he said.

Jim reeled back as though struck. 'Michael . . . is that you?'

'Long time no see, Jim,' said Michael. 'You ain't changed a bit.'

Jim waded into the water until he was face to face with this man who was saying he was his own flesh and blood.

'Michael? What's happened to you? You're just skin and bone.'

'Guess I've lost a few pounds . . . '

'And your face . . . '

'Ain't nobody shaves round these parts.'

'How long have you been here?'

Suddenly, Michael looked desperately tired. 'Look, Jim, I'd like to talk but I gotta get back to my claim and I ain't ate for a few days so maybe some other time . . . thanks for the money, though.'

Jim grabbed his arm. 'Wait, Michael. I came all this way to find you. I got something to tell you.'

'So tell me . . . but make it quick.'

74

'Let me buy you a coffee and some chow.'

'Can't spare the diggin' time, Jim.'

'This is important. It's about Ma.'

Michael hesitated and rubbed his beard.

'OK. Reckon I could spare a few minutes since you came all this way.'

'Let's go back to town.'

Michael smiled broadly. 'Well, c'mon brother. Don't stand gawpin' at me as though I was a ghost. Let's get some grub and you can tell me just what is so goddamned important!'

10

Craven sat back in his leather chair and stared at his office door long after Edith had left. He reached forward to a mahogany box and removed a cigar. Still staring at the door, he bit off its end and carefully lit it. A cloud of blue smoke swirled up towards the roof as he considered his next move.

There was no doubt in his mind that one day Edith would be his. The only questions were 'how' and 'when'. He was still searching for the answers when a knock on the door disturbed his thoughts.

'Come in,' he called irritably.

'All alone?' asked Kid Cassidy.

Craven nodded and pushed the open cigar box in the Kid's direction.

'Don't mind if I do,' said the Kid. He helped himself, then sat across from Craven, who waited until his cigar was well lit.

'D'you find Payne?' he said eventually.

The young gunman shook his head. 'Wasn't at the Tuckered Out. Word is someone saw him making his way down to the river. I put a couple of the boys on to it. As soon as they find him they'll come and get me.'

Craven nodded and clenched his cigar tightly between his teeth. Minutes passed before he spoke again.

'Well? Go ahead and say it.'

'Say what?'

'The kind of thing you usually say when me and Edith have had one of our discussions.'

The Kid smiled. 'I've said all I'm gonna say, Cole. You know how I feel about her. I think she's bad news. We should have got rid of her the same time we got rid of her old man.'

'That's not going to happen.'

'You know, this would be a whole lot easier if you hadn't gone and fallen in love with her.'

Craven stared at him. 'Whether it's love or not, she's gonna be mine. I just don't know what she wants!'

'Maybe she doesn't want anything.'

'Everybody wants something. Everybody's got a price. I just don't know what hers is!'

'Beats me,' said the Kid, flicking the ash from his cigar. 'Reckon you'd have to ask the new boy in town. Maybe she wants him.'

Craven's eyes narrowed. 'What d'ya mean?'

'You weren't there, Cole. You didn't see the way she looked at him. You didn't see the way she stepped in between us to make sure I didn't plug the guy. Yes, sirree, I reckon you got some competition there.'

As soon as the Kid uttered the words, he regretted it. He looked across at Craven apprehensively.

'You know, I like you, Kid,' said Craven quietly, 'but don't go pushing my tolerance. You're outta line. Hear me?'

'OK. I'm sorry. Forgot you were so touchy about the girl.'

Craven stubbed out his cigar and glowered at the Kid through the cloud of smoke that hung over his desk like a bad mood.

'Let's get down to business. I've made a decision. It's time to quit Golden Gulch.'

'It's time to what?' exclaimed the Kid.

'A good gambler knows when to cash in. How long do you think we can go on milking this town? We're getting to the end, Kid. I got an instinct for these things.'

'What things?' asked the Kid.

'Too many people are beginning to smell a rat. I'm hearing talk. Then this guy Payne shows up and starts sniffing around the river. He's looking for something. I don't like it.'

'When do we go?'

'End of the week. We'll salt the river again tonight. We'll leave Jamieson in charge and by the time the gold runs out we'll have set up somewhere else, upriver.'

'What about Edith?'

'She's coming with us.'

'Did she say that?'

'She doesn't know yet.'

The Kid smiled. 'And what about Payne?'

'Keep an eye on him but don't kill him until I say the word. I got a feeling he'll come in useful before we fix him for good.'

11

Dusty Murphy and the Payne brothers sat near the back of the Tuckered Out Café. Tommy was wiping down some tables when Dusty called the boy over.

'Your mom not around?'

'Ain't back from the Blood & Sweat yet.'

Jim noticed the boy's fair hair and blue eyes and couldn't help noting how much he resembled his mom. He was a boy most men would have been proud to call 'son'.

'What can I get ya?'

'Coffee for Dusty and me. Full works for my brother here.'

As Tommy went to get their order, Dusty looked from one to the other of the two men sitting across from him. They were brothers, sure enough. Same height, same build, but that was where the similarity ended. Even though the

81

same blood might have coursed through their veins, the two men couldn't have been more different. Just as quickly as he had taken an instant liking to Jim, he felt the opposite towards his brother.

When the food arrived Jim and Dusty watched Michael devour his pig and beans as though it was the last meal he would ever have on this earth. When Michael had wiped the tin plate clean with a chunk of bread he leaned back in the chair contentedly and rubbed his hands over his ribs.

'Well, that sure filled a hole.' He smiled. 'Say, one of you fellas wouldn't have a smoke, would you?'

Jim reached into the inside of his vest and offered his brother a cheroot. Michael lit it and drew heavily. He leaned back in his chair, closed his eyes and blew a large cloud of smoke into the air above him. Then he suddenly leaned forward.

'So, how ya been, little brother?'

'I've been OK.'

'Still a lawman?'

'You're a lawman?' Dusty almost shouted.

Jim looked around urgently. 'I'd appreciate it if that just stayed at this table, if you don't mind.'

'So — what's this 'bout Ma?' said Michael.

'If this is family business, I can go,' said Dusty making to stand up.

'No, you're fine, Dusty,' said Jim. He reached into the top pocket of his shirt and pulled out the grubby letter. 'I promised her I'd hand this letter to you personally.'

He placed it carefully on the table. Michael stared at it for a few moments.

'You've come a long way just to deliver a letter,' he murmured.

'I promised Ma I would.'

'And you always keep your promises. You always were a good boy, weren't you, Jim?' Michael sneered. 'Always Ma's favourite weren't you?'

'She's got no favourites.'

'I was Pa's,' said Michael, anger

flaring in his eyes, 'until you let him die!'

Dusty rose to go.

'Look, fellas, you got family business here and I really think I — '

'Sit down, old man,' said Michael. 'It's all right. It's history now. Just thought you should know what sort of fella you've hitched up with. Your pal here left our pa to die in a barn fire.'

'That's a lie! I tried to save him!'

'You left him to burn!'

'I told you a million times. He was trapped under the plough. I tried to get it off him. I was only a kid.'

'You didn't try hard enough!'

'He told me to go.'

'We've only your word for that.'

'Don't you think I think about it all the time? Don't you think I go over that night again and again wonderin' if there was something else I could've done? Don't you think I think about it every time I look at this?' said Jim as, fiercely, he pulled the glove from his right hand.

Dusty stared at what at once had

been a human hand. It was hardly more than a stump, the fingers melted together in a stiff clump of burn-scarred flesh. Only the thumb was still useable, like the pincer of a crab. Jim held his hand out in front of his brother, then realizing his hand was in full view, he awkwardly slid the glove back on, hiding it once more, ashamed of its uselessness, aware of how it had failed him in the past.

Dusty knew he was witnessing an argument that had been played out many times. He cleared his throat.

'Say, Michael, don't you want to know what's in the letter?'

'Ask Jim.'

'I don't know what it says.'

'You don't know? All that way and all that time on your hands and you were never once tempted to have a look inside?'

'Ma sealed it. If she had wanted me to know she would have told me.'

Michael smiled. 'No wonder they made you sheriff. Surprised you ain't a saint by now. But say, I noticed you ain't wearing your piece of tin. You were normally so proud of that thing, strutting up and down our home town. What's wrong, Mr Lawman? Golden Gulch a bit rough for you?'

'Read the letter, Michael. Read the letter so I can go home.'

Michael lifted the letter and started to tear the edges. Then he stopped.

'You bumped into Kid Cassidy yet? He works for a fella name of Coleridge Craven. These two fellas got this place sewn up tight between them. In fact, this place here belongs to his girl. She's real pretty, but out of bounds, if you know what I mean. I was thinkin' that maybe Craven might not be too happy with a lawman in his town. He's mighty generous to folks who look out for his interests. Maybe I should let him know about you . . . '

Suddenly, Jim grabbed his gun and, below the table, rammed the barrel of his Dragoon deep into his brother's ribs.

'Listen to me, Michael,' he hissed, 'I

didn't come all this way just so you could threaten me. I promised Ma I'd get this letter to you but I don't want to be around you one more minute than I have to and I guess you feel the same way. So read the goddam letter or God help me it'll be the last thing you do!'

Wincing with the pain of the steel in his ribs, Michael unfolded the thin sheets of paper.

'You know my readin' ain't good. Spent too much time away from the schoolhouse.'

'You read, Dusty?' asked Payne.

'Sure, I can read,' said Dusty indignantly.

He scrabbled in his shirt pocket and took out a pair of thin gold-wired spectacles which he carefully wrapped around his ears. He took the letter and cleared his throat.

My Darling Son, Michael,
If you are reading this it means
that Jim has done his duty as I
knew he would and has delivered it

safely into your hands. I don't know where he has tracked you down but I pray that you are safe and well. I've been so worried about you since you disappeared all these months back with no word or letter where you were going to. Rumour was that you had headed off on some foolish notion of finding gold!

I know things have been hard for you since your daddy died. I don't think you ever got over that. And I don't think you ever stopped blaming Jim, but there was nothing more that boy could have done. I cannot tell you what it does to a mother to watch her two sons tear each other apart when you were once so close.

I have so much to talk to you about but I need to get to the reason for this letter. A couple of months ago I was feeling real poorly. Eventually I had to go see Doc Brimley. He told me I have *the cancer. He can't tell exactly how long I got left but he reckons I'm into my last six months. I want to see you before I die. I want to see you one last time and tell you how sorry I am I couldn't be a mother and father to you both. And I wanted one last time to see you and Jim together as loving brothers the way you both used to be before that terrible fire took your daddy from us.*

I am praying that you will heed the wishes of a dying woman and do this last thing for me. Come home with your brother. I will wait here as long as I can but I do not know how long God will spare me.

I love you and miss you,
Your loving Mother.

'That's all there is, boys,' said Dusty, removing his spectacles.

'Why didn't you tell me she was dying?' whispered Michael.

Jims face was ashen white. 'I didn't

know. I knew she'd been poorly but I didn't know she was dying.'

'Would you have left her if you'd known?' asked Dusty.

'Of course I wouldn't have,' said Payne.

'Then I reckon that's why she didn't tell you.'

Payne suddenly rose to his feet. 'I gotta go. I've wasted enough time. I've gotta get back.'

'You goin' with him?' said Dusty to Michael.

Michael took the folded letter from Dusty's hand and put it in his top pocket. 'Sure, I'll come with you. I just need to get some things together.'

'We need to be out of here before sundown,' said Payne.

'Won't take me long. I ain't got much. Most of my gear was sold or stolen. But I owe somebody some cash. I need to come to an arrangement with him.'

'OK. I'll meet you back here in two hours,' said Payne, and he turned to go.

'Jim?' said Michael.

'Yeah?'

'I guess I just wanted to say — ' but Michael's words were drowned out as gunshots rang out in the street. Every miner in the café was on their feet and running out on to the sidewalk. The three men followed them.

The street was filled with hollering and shouting and firearms were being let off as though it was the fourth of July. The sidewalks were packed as they ran in the direction of the river and those who couldn't get on the sidewalks were making their way as best they could down the main street, some falling and wallowing in the mud.

'What's going on?' shouted Jim above the fray.

'They hit pay dirt!' yelled Michael as he made to join the crowd. Jim grabbed his arm

'Where are you goin'?'

Michael's eyes were wide and wild. 'Where am I going? Are you crazy? Where do you think I'm going? I'm going to get me some gold!'

Jims grip grew tighter. 'But what about Ma?'

A flicker of doubt passed over his brother's face. 'Ma? Oh, yeah, Ma. Sure. Look, Jim, you go home. I'll follow you. I'll be home as soon as I can. Tell her to hold on for me.'

'Hold on for you?' said Jim in disbelief.

'Yeah, and tell her, when I get home I'll be able to get her the best doctors money can buy. I'll set her up in a new place with help so she won't have to work so hard ever again. Tell her I'll buy her pretty dresses and I'll — '

'Pretty dresses? She's *dying*, Michael, your ma's dyin . . . '

Michael slipped his grasp from his arm and started running towards the river. Jim watched for a few minutes but soon he was lost in the torrent of men.

Payne felt he had lost him for ever.

12

Jim and Dusty watched the river of miners pass the Tuckered Out Café.

'What is it that drives men crazy like that, Dusty?'

Dusty removed his hat and scratched the top of his head.

'It's the gold fever. I seen it before though I ain't seen it in so many so bad.' He shook his head. 'Weren't like this in the old days.'

'I did what I said I'd do. I can't do no more,' said Jim almost to himself.

'What you figurin' on doin' now?'

'My job's done, Dusty. I gave him the letter. Can't drag him with me. If kin don't mean nothing next to a handful of gold, there's nothing I can do about it.'

'Think yourself lucky you know the difference.'

'Think so? Guess we're all guilty of

wanting something we can't have. Reckon we've all chased fool's gold at some part of our lives.'

'You gonna go home now?'

'Nothin' here for me now. I'll get my things and make tracks. Ma'll be waitin' for me. Don't know how I'm gonna break it to her when I turn up empty-handed. Reckon if the cancer don't kill her, a broken heart surely will.'

Dusty smiled and put a hand on Jim's shoulder.

'Well, at least she's got one good boy she can be proud of.'

'Thanks, Dusty. Best be on my way.'

'Say, I got an idea!' said Dusty and grabbed Jim's arm. 'Reckon I could knock some sense into your brother.'

'How?'

'Well, I told you. All this gold stuff is a scam! There ain't no real gold there. It's just Craven saltin' the river. I told you all about it. You help me blow this wide open and your brother'll have nothin' to stay here for. Once I prove there ain't no gold, these men'll scatter to the four winds like tumbleweed. You could help me do it!'

Jim shook his head and smiled.

'You're crazier than they are. You don't give up, do you? I don't have time to help you fight your battles. Take my advice, Dusty. You get yourself back up into the hills and pick up where you left your quiet life. You don't belong here any more'n I do. These crazy sons-abitches ain't worth gettin' killed for. Think you can take Craven and his men on single-handed?'

'Nope, not me. You could, though,' said Dusty, glancing sideways at Jim.

'Maybe you're right but I don't intend to find out. I've told you, Dusty. This ain't my fight. And it ain't yours neither. Forget it.'

Dusty sighed and beat his hat against his thigh, sending out a cloud of dust. 'I guess you're right at that,' he said.

'Anyway,' said Jim, holding out his hand, 'thanks for helping me find

Michael. So long, Dusty. You take care of yourself.'

Dusty took Jim's hand and shook it warmly.

'So long, Jim. I doubt our paths'll ever cross again but it was nice knowing ya awhile. Don't be too hard on your brother. It ain't really his fault. It's the gold fever.'

'Sure. I know. Thanks.'

The two men parted and walked off in opposite directions.

As Dusty walked towards the river he looked over his shoulder and saw Jim cross the muddy street towards the Blood & Sweat saloon. Dusty didn't get to meet many good men in his line of work, so he recognized one when he saw one. He knew it might be a long time before he met one again.

As he made his way to fetch his mule and pack his things, he passed a blind preacher standing on an old packing-case, quoting the Book of Revelations.

And I looked, and behold a pale horse and his name that sat on him was

Death and Hell followed with him. And power was given unto them over the fourth part of the earth to kill with sword . . .

Dusty sighed. Jim was right. He didn't belong here among all this madness. He needed fresh mountain air and his own company for a while.

★   ★   ★

Jim heard the preacher too as he stood at the entrance to the Blood & Sweat Saloon and tried to scrape the mud from his boots. He was sick of the stuff and was looking forward to getting back on to solid ground. As he put his hand on the batwing doors, he heard someone whisper his name.

'Mr Payne?'

He looked around. He couldn't see anyone. He turned again.

'Mr Payne!' This time the voice was more urgent. 'Over here.'

Stacked outside the hotel was a pile of barrels marked 'Champagne,

France', although Jim suspected their contents had been made in some back alley not far from where he stood. Jim reached for his gun, cocked the hammer and looked behind the barrels. He recognized the shock of blond hair.

'What you doin', boy?'

'Mom told me to give you this.'

Tommy thrust a piece of folded paper into Jim's hand, then sprinted off down the street in the direction of the Tuckered Out Café. Jim smiled as he watched the boy disappear, uncocked his gun and let the weapon slide back into the holster. Checking he wasn't being watched, he opened the note.

Dear Mr Payne,
Forgive me writing to you this way but it is important I meet with you at the café tonight. I want to thank you for what you did today and also to tell you that you are in grave danger. If you do not come, I will understand and I wish you well for your future. Whatever you

decide to do, you must leave Golden Gulch soon. Please destroy this note after you read it. Do not tell anyone of our meeting,

Yours,
Edith Winsome.

Jim read the note three times before folding it and sliding it into his top pocket. As he went into the Blood & Sweat he wondered how many more surprises Golden Gulch had in store for him.

13

A few hours later Jim stood in his room and surveyed himself in the mirror.

Although he would never have admitted it, he had taken a little more time over his appearance than normal. He took out Edith's note for the twentieth time, read it, then folded it and tucked it into his top shirt pocket where he kept his neckerchief.

With a clean shirt and pants and a close shave, he felt human again. He lifted his sheriff's badge from the top of the drawer and pinned it under the lapel of his vest. After one last check, Jim left his room and made his way along the narrow corridor. He'd been lucky to get a room. Everywhere else was full. He'd winced a little when the desk clerk had told him the price of an overnight stay but, after weeks of sleeping under a tarp, he reckoned he was due a little luxury.

At the top of the stairs he paused, surveying the scene below him. The saloon sure had pretensions to grandeur. Nubile young women painted in the Greek style decorated the walls, blatant enough to make new arrivals blush with embarrassment. Below the landing where he stood Jim watched the roulette wheel with the golden spike in the middle. A crowd of men were gathered around it, throwing chips on the table, and Jim wondered what made a man do back-breaking work for days then risk it all on the spin of a wheel.

Faro and poker games were going on at tables scattered around the bar and a piano-player in the corner tried valiantly to be heard above the raucous noise. Men stood three deep at the bar and Jim couldn't help but notice that their favourite tipple was champagne.

He made his way down the stairs and headed for the batwing doors. As he passed the bar he heard a voice he recognized.

'Care to join me for a drink, brother?' Jim turned and saw Michael leaning against the bar, each arm draped across the bare shoulders of a prairie nymph. He was dressed in a freshly pressed suit, his hair was slicked back and his beard was neatly trimmed. 'My money's good if that's what's worrying you!'

He went into his waistcoat pocket and placed a small canvas bag with a drawstring in the middle of his palm. The two girls cuddled closer to him, staring at the bag as though hypnotized.

'Can't believe you almost talked me into leaving this place. Soon as I got myself down to that river I struck it lucky. Must've hauled out a couple of hundred dollars worth out there today. Going back tomorrow for some more.'

'You sure there is more?' asked Jim.

'Plenty.'

'Well, good luck with that.' Jim made to walk past his brother but Michael put his boot out to bar his way.

'Now, come on, Jim. This is no way for brothers to part. Seems the least you can do is admit you were wrong. Let's at least have a drink for old time's sake. You can tell Ma when you saw me I was doing well. She'd like that. She could die happy!'

'Why don't you tell her yourself?' said Jim quietly.

'You just can't be happy for me, can you? Now I've got a bit of success here, you just can't bear to see me doing better than you, can you?'

'You seem to have gotten this idea into your fool head that in some way I'm jealous of you. I wouldn't trade places with you for all the gold you think lies in that river out yonder. Tomorrow, I'll be gone and if we're both lucky, you won't ever have to set eyes on me again and that'll be the end of that. So move your boot so I can be on my way.'

Michael's mouth tightened into a thin line of anger. 'You know what, little brother? I oughtta take you outside and give you the whupping I used to when we were kids.'

'You're welcome to try but just in case you haven't noticed, I'm not a kid any more.'

Michael took a step towards him. 'Why, I oughtta . . . '

Jim pulled back the hammer on the Dragoon. 'Don't even think about it. I'm looking for any excuse to blow your damn fool head off. Now get out of my way while you still can.'

Reluctantly, Michael stepped back and Jim walked towards the saloon door.

'You think I'm finished with you?' Michael shouted after him. 'You think you're just gonna ride out of here as though nothin's happened? Your day of reckonin's comin', sooner'n you think!'

Jim pushed straight through the doors and stood on the front porch. The night was warm and he pulled his neckerchief from his top pocket to wipe the back of his neck. He didn't notice Edith's note falling on to the wooden sidewalk. As he made his way towards the Tuckered Out Café, the saloon doors opened again. The Kid came out, noticed the piece of paper on the sidewalk and lifted it.

'Well, well,' he said quietly as he read it. He'd watched the argument in the bar between the two brothers and had heard Michael threaten his brother in front of a room full of witnesses.

He was smiling as he turned back into the saloon to find Craven.

14

Dusty had his old mule, Patsy, packed and ready to go in less than an hour after he'd said goodbye to Jim. He worked with the speed of a man with no roots and used to breaking camp quickly and if he hadn't bumped into Seamus Kilpatrick, he could have put half a day's distance between himself and Golden Gulch. Seamus was an old-timer like himself, he and Dusty went back a long way. He was adamant Dusty would not leave the town without a farewell whiskey or two.

By the time they had got through half a bottle of red-eye, reminisced about the good old days and swapped stories about the fortunes of mutual friends, dusk was rolling in. By the time Dusty passed the town boundaries, it was dark.

He knew it wasn't a good time to hit

the trail but there would be a full moon and he trusted Patsy. Besides, he didn't intend to go far; he just didn't want to spend another night in Golden Gulch. It would have been too easy to stay in the saloon with Seamus and let the gut-rot whiskey warm his belly, but he knew if he didn't leave tonight, he might never go.

Maybe it was the whiskey but Dusty felt better with every step he put between him and the town and he began to remember how much he didn't mind his own company. He found himself thinking about Jim Payne and his brother and the more he thought about it, the more he realized that the younger man was right. Proving that Craven was salting the river wasn't his problem any more. What those greenhorns chose to believe or not was none of his damn business. That was what towns did to you with all their bustle and noise. They muddled your thinking.

Dusty followed the river upstream

and by the time he had reckoned he had covered a mile or so he started looking for somewhere to bed down for the night.

He came to a wide bend in the river where there were large boulders along the bank.

'Looks a good as place as any, Patsy my old girl,' said Dusty and the mule obediently came to a halt.

With a groan, Dusty swung his stiff leg over the head of the beast and started removing the saddlebags that were draped over it. He found a large overhanging rock and he settled under it. Although the riverbank was stony there was a large bed of sand under the rocks. It was warm and dry and if it happened to rain tonight, the overhanging rock would give him shelter. As he unrolled his tarp and cooking pans, Dusty could hear the gentle splash and gurgle of the wide river not far from him.

He quickly gathered a few armfuls of driftwood while Patsy wandered down to the river's edge to drink her fill. In no time at all he had a fire going in the middle of the small circle of stones he'd made. Later, when the fire had faded to embers, he would wrap the stones under his tarp and their heat would keep him warm during the cold night.

When he went down to the river and scooped a pan of water, Patsy lazily raised her head.

'Let's make sure you don't go wandering off, now,' said Dusty and he pulled the mule up to a large clump of bushes. As he tied up her reins, the mule started stripping leaves.

Back at the fire, Dusty lit his pipe and stared into the yellow flames; he felt more content than he had for a long time. Yessir, this was what life was going to be like from now on in.

He rested his eyes, then, just as he was about to doze off, he heard voices.

Dusty wasn't easily spooked but something about the sound of those voices out here in the middle of nowhere made him sit bolt upright. He quickly scooped sand over the fire which died quickly with hardly any smoke. The voices were pretty close now but Dusty knew he was well hidden below the overhanging rock. All the same, he felt a tight knot in the pit of his stomach and he realized that his heart was racing. He heard boots and hoofs above his head and he pushed himself against the back of the rock, pulling his legs in under his body. He glanced over to the bush where Patsy was tied fearing she would give him away, but the mule stood motionless in the cool night air and was almost invisible to the strangers.

The men and their mounts crossed the rock above Dusty's head and made their way down a shallow bank to the water's edge. Dusty rolled over and lay flat on his belly, trying to make himself as small as possible, so that if the men turned around they would not see him in the shadows.

From his vantage point Dusty could see two men clearly. Both were tall and thick set and Dusty recognized them as part of Kid Cassidy's outfit. There were three horses, one being used as a packhorse with two small nail-kegs slung over the saddle.

Dusty now had a decision to make; one that his life might depend on. Should he lie low and wait for the men to finish their business and go, or should he try to get to Patsy and put as much distance between them as he could? Just as he was weighing up his options, the two men interrupted his thoughts.

'Get the kegs, Chuck,' ordered one of the men who, Dusty could now see, was older with silver sideburns.

Chuck did as he was told and lifted down the two small barrels. He tucked them under each arm, took them to the older man at the water's edge and dumped them on the stony bank. Crouching down, he knocked out the stoppers, tipped one of the barrels to one side and let some of the contents drain into his hand. Gold dust sparked in the moonlight. Dusty's eyes opened wide.

'Seems a shame to go throwing this into the river, don't it?' said Chuck.

'Don't start gettin' no smart ideas, will ya? The boss wants all this gold in the river tonight . . . and he means all of it. If he even suspected you was thinkin' of takin' a cut there'd be hell to pay!'

'Come on, Hank, he ain't gonna miss the odd handful, is he?'

'Listen to me, son. I've been working with Craven and the Kid since this whole thing kicked off, and I don't know how they do it but they got eyes and ears everywhere. How do I know they've not put you up to this to see what I say? Come to that, how do you know I ain't gonna let you put some in your pocket and then tell 'em as soon as I get back to town?'

Chuck stared at the older man for a few moments before letting the grains of gold slide back into the barrel. 'Just seems a shame. That's all I was sayin'.'

'You ain't paid to think,' said Hank. 'Now, if you've got over your foolish notions, let's get on with what we get paid to do.'

The two men lifted a barrel each and waded out until the water was over their knees. They started tipping the gold into the water.

Dusty watched intently. Now he had seen it with his own eyes and he had caught Craven's men red-handed. If he could get back to town and get Seamus and some of the men, they could come up here and bushwhack these crooks. They might have finished salting the river by then, but if they could be caught before they got back to town, they could get them to confess in front of witnesses. Then they could run Craven out of town.

Dusty looked over at Patsy. He guessed the distance to cover and reckoned he could manage it without getting caught. Any noise he might make, he hoped would be covered by the sound of the running water.

He waited another few minutes, making sure the men were intent on their business before he made his move. Keeping well into the shadows, he stepped across the stony ground hardly daring to breathe. He made slow but steady progress and was soon only about six feet or so away from the mule. Suddenly, she let out a small bray of alarm and stamped a hoof nervously, causing a small clatter of stones.

'Hear that?' said Chuck.

'Hear what?' Hank stopped pouring the gold and listened.

'Thought I heard something.'

'Naw,' said Hank eventually, 'can't hear nothin'. Gettin' mighty jumpy, ain't ya?'

'Just wanna make sure there's nobody out there,' said Chuck. 'If word got back 'bout what we're doin' those miners would string us up!'

'Relax. Nobody's gonna find out. Come on, let's get this over and done with and get back to town.'

The two men started pouring the gold again.

Dusty stood stock still and cursed the mule under his breath. He didn't know how long he stayed motionless but not until he was sure Craven's men were not on their way to investigate did he dare to move again.

He looked towards the river. He could just make out the men's outlines in the water and he breathed a shallow sigh of relief. He turned towards Patsy again and this time, the animal was looking straight at him. Reassured that the thing coming through the dark wasn't a rattlesnake or a coyote, when Dusty moved towards her she didn't stir. He reached out and patted her neck.

'Listen to me, my old sweetheart,' he whispered, 'you make a noise and you'll be liable to get us both killed.'

Slowly, he untied the reins from the bush and gently pulled on them. His plan was to lead the mule until he was sure he was out of earshot, then swing himself across her back and get back to town as quickly as possible. He pulled on the halter, then stopped as the mule let out a loud and frightened bray. A figure had stepped out of the darkness and it was pointing a gun at Dusty's head.

'That's about as far as you're goin' tonight, mister,' said Kid Cassidy. 'Hank? Chuck? Get over here!'

Dusty raised his hands. Behind him he heard the two men splash out of the river and run up the bank. They were almost as shocked to see the Kid as Dusty had been.

'Kid,' spluttered Hank, 'what are you doing here?'

The Kid smiled without taking his eyes off Dusty. 'You know I like to keep an eye on things. You didn't think I was gonna let you boys ride out of town with a fortune in gold and not check that it all went where it was meant to go?' He glanced across at Chuck. 'That amount of gold can tempt a man sorely.'

116

Chuck swallowed hard. 'Kid, I was only joshin' . . . I wasn't gonna — '

'Shuddup,' snarled Kid Cassidy. 'We'll talk about that later. Right now, we got this fella to deal with.'

The three men looked at Dusty.

'So, how much did you see, old man?' asked Hank eventually.

'Nothin',' mumbled Dusty, 'I didn't see nothin' . . . honest.'

'I think you saw enough,' said the Kid. 'Enough for us not to let you get back to Golden Gulch and start shootin' your mouth off.'

Dusty's heart sank. He had never pretended to be a brave man. 'I won't tell anyone! I was leavin' Golden Gulch anyway. I ain't never goin' back!'

Chuck wiped the back of his hand across his dried lips. 'What we gonna do, Kid?'

'I think you know what we gotta do.'

The young man hesitated, looking at the Kid and Hank in turn, and then stared at Dusty.

'What's the matter?' drawled the Kid,

'ain't you ever killed a man before? You don't seem so cocky now. An hour ago you were thinkin' of helpin' yourself to Craven's gold and now it looks like you can't do the job he was payin' you for.'

Chuck's face had gone pale in the night. 'Just because I ain't killed a man don't mean I can't,' he protested weakly.

'Well, now's your chance. I gotta know I can trust you, Chuck. I gotta know you're up to the job. Cos if you're not, seems to me you're in the same position as this old man here. Know what I mean?'

'You can trust me, Kid!' said Chuck nervously.

The Kid smiled and pushed his hat to the back of his head.

'OK. Let's see you plug 'im.' He smiled across at Hank. 'It's a lot easier when they ain't shootin' back, ain't it?'

Dusty listened to the conversation between the men. He couldn't believe he was going to die but he watched in terror as the young man nervously pulled out his gun. The Kid and Hank took a few paces back.

Chuck raised his firearm and pointed it at Dusty's chest. Dusty saw the beads of perspiration on the young man's brow and noticed that the barrel of the gun was shaking in his trembling hand. For a split second Dusty almost felt sorry for him — but this might just give him the chance he needed. Dusty could see tears in the boy's eyes which meant that he would be just a blurred shadow. Just as Chuck started to exert the required pressure on the trigger, he closed his eyes — and that was Dusty's chance.

Dusty wheeled and dived into the bushes just as the darkness was lit by the flash of gunfire. There was shouting behind him as he plunged through the vegetation in pitch blackness.

He could hear the men cursing and shouting behind him and shots were fired wildly around but none came close. Just as he thought he was going to make it, he felt a dull thud in the back of his shoulder.

He keeled over, falling heavily on to the stony riverbank and rolled on to his back, gasping for breath. The last thing he saw were the stars in the sky before his eyes closed and the darkness engulfed him.

15

The Tuckered Out Café was empty and almost in darkness. The dim halo of a kerosene lamp turned down low lit a single table. Payne sat alone holding a cup of coffee, enjoying the stillness, and felt a warm contentment spread through him. The coffee was hot and strong and nicely finished the meal that Edith had cooked for them.

Edith came out from the back room. 'He's sleeping now', she said as she sat across from him.

'He's a fine boy,' said Payne.

She smiled, unable to hide the pride that lit her eyes. 'Yes, he is,' she said. 'If it wasn't for him I don't know if I could have carried on. There wouldn't have been any point.'

'Is he like his pa?' asked Payne.

Edith looked up a little too sharply, unable to hide the suspicion in her eyes.

121

'In what way, Mr Payne?'

'I'm sorry . . . I didn't mean to pry . . . I simply meant . . . '

Edith suddenly smiled. 'No, it's me who's sorry. I didn't mean to snap at you. I guess things are still a little raw.'

'You don't have to talk about it if you don't want to.'

They sat in silence but Jim found it agreeable, not awkward at all; the way he sometimes felt with other women. He found Edith easy to be with. His thoughts began to drift again and when he looked up, she was staring quizzically at him.

'You were miles away.'

'Sorry. I was thinking about something else.'

Edith smiled. 'You're a strange one, Mr Payne, aren't you?'

'How so?'

'Oh, I don't know. Maybe I've been surrounded too long by too many men who were only interested in what they could get for themselves. They call it 'getting on' or 'making it' or even 'progress' but it all boils down to one thing at the end of the day — and that's greed. After a while it gets pretty ugly.'

'Guess I've always had a place to rest my head and I've seldom gone hungry. How much more does a man need?'

Through the soft light of the kerosene lamp, Edith looked intently into Jim's eyes. She was about to say something, then seemed to change her mind. She stood up and started gathering the plates. 'Well, this ain't getting the washing-up done.'

'I'll help,' said Jim rising to his feet.

'No, you sit where you are. I'll have this done in no time.'

'Mind if I smoke?'

'Go right ahead,' she said as she went through to the kitchen. As she went, Jim noticed three carpetbags sitting packed at the door but decided it was none of his business to enquire about them.

He lit a cigar and watched the smoke rise into the darkness. When the table was cleared, Edith returned to her chair.

'So what was it you wanted to talk to me about?' asked Jim.

'Well, I wanted to thank you for what you did today; for trying to stop the Kid. For stepping in when Tommy got hurt.'

'Anybody would have done it.'

'Not anybody in Golden Gulch.'

'I thought you were angry at me.'

'I was, but only because I didn't want to see another good man get killed.'

She looked at him intently. 'You do know, Mr Payne, that you're on the wrong side of Craven and the Kid. They'll try to make sure you don't leave Golden Gulch alive.'

'I'm leavin' tonight.'

'I'm glad to hear it,' said Edith, although her voice lacked conviction.

There was a pause before Jim said, 'The only thing I don't understand is . . . ' then he stopped.

'What were you going to say?' asked Edith.

'No, ma'am. It's none of my business.'

'You were going to ask me what I was doing mixed up with the likes of Craven, weren't you?'

'I'd be a liar if I said it hadn't crossed my mind.'

Edith sat back in the chair and sighed.

'We came to Golden Gulch just after gold had been found. We had a little ranch up in Montana, Jack, my husband, Tommy and me. Our spread wasn't big but we got by and we were happy. Jack loved his horses and he seemed to have everything he wanted until he heard about the gold. The idea got into his head and he couldn't shake it. It was all he spoke about until nothing would stop him coming. He said we would regret it for the rest of our lives if we stayed where we were. He reckoned in a few months we'd strike it rich and then we'd buy a big ranch with the biggest house I'd ever seen, with ranch hands and maids to help out. I didn't want any of those things but he never asked me.'

'Sounds like he had the gold fever.'

'He sure had. I thought he'd gone mad until I came here and saw that same wild look in everybody's eyes and heard all that talk about gold and money.'

'So you came to Golden Gulch.'

Edith looked down at the table and started following the grain of the wood with a fingernail.

'We sold everything. The ranch, the horses, everything. Jack put all the money he had into supplies and tools. Two months went past and he found nothing. Nobody did. The only person making money here was Craven. Then Jack started getting bitter and angry. Word went round that Craven was salting the river, so Jack persuaded the other miners to take a stand against him.'

'What happened?'

'One night, coming home from a secret meeting, he was gunned down from behind by one of Craven's men, although I couldn't prove it.'

'So why did you stay?'

'I had nowhere to go. No money. I had Tommy to think of. Then Craven came around and said he felt bad about what happened to Jack. He said he would look after me with no strings attached. Pretty soon he set me up in this place and I've done pretty well.' Edith laughed bitterly. 'I've made more than Jack ever did. But a man like Craven does nothin' for nothin'.'

'I guess not.'

'Craven thinks I owe him. He won't be happy until we're married.'

'And will you?'

Edith looked straight into Jim's face.

'I won't lie. I've thought about it. But if I did, it would be for all the wrong reasons. So, no, Mr Payne. I will not marry Coleridge Craven. Despite what he thinks, not everything's for sale.'

Edith's gaze turned towards the kitchen.

'We've packed our bags.'

'I noticed.'

'We're leaving tonight. Nobody knows but you, but I didn't want to leave without saying thank you.'

'I appreciate it,'

Edith looked around the café. 'This will be the last meal I cook in The Tuckered Out. At least I can remember it as a pleasant one.'

Embarrassed, Jim took out his pocket watch.

'It's past midnight. I should go.'

Edith nodded and followed him to the door. 'Thank you, Mr Payne.'

'You've thanked me already.'

'No, this time I'm thanking you for tonight. For giving me some hope that there are some decent men left out there.'

Jim smiled awkwardly. 'There's plenty of us.'

'Take care of yourself,' said Edith as he opened the door. Then he hesitated.

'Edith, I . . . ' he began, then stopped.

'Yes?' she said searching his face.

'I was going to ask . . . '

'What?'

Jim paused, struggling for words and then shook his head.

'It's nothing. You take care of yourself, too. Say goodbye to Tommy for me,' he said and walked out on to the boardwalk.

As he heard the door lock behind him he lit a cheroot. For a moment he had the strange urge to go back and knock on the door. If they were both leaving, then why not leave together? But if Edith had wanted that, she would have said. She was running away from the unwanted attentions of a man. She didn't want another one foisted upon her.

In frustration, he threw the half-smoked cigar into the mud, then started to walk towards the Blood & Sweat. He sensed rather than heard someone behind him but before he could turn around, he felt a sickening thud on the back of his head and he plunged into darkness.

16

Slowly, Dusty opened his eyes but all he could see was blackness so he presumed he was dead.

There was a dull, painful roaring in his ears and he lay on his back wondering what the noise could be. It grew louder and louder, then softened and faded until it was almost pleasant and he recognized it as the sound of a river.

He tried to move, then groaned in agony as a sharp pain shot through his back, taking his breath away. He decided not to try again for a while.

He remembered the roar of a gun and bright flashes ripping through the night as he ran through bushes. He recalled the crippling pain as he felt a bullet go through his shoulder. Then it all became a blur. The last thing he remembered was crashing face down on to the stony riverbank and then falling down a dark, bottomless hole.

As he lay there trying to piece it altogether, his eyes started to pick out small specks of light shimmering in the blackness and he realized that they were stars. A cold wind passed over him and he shivered. He didn't think a corpse could feel the cold so maybe he wasn't dead after all!

He tried to swallow but found his throat so parched it felt as if it was lined with sand, and the sound of running water so close made him even thirstier. As he started to think of how he could get down to the water's edge, he wondered whether his killers were still out there somewhere.

His eyes were now growing accustomed to the darkness. He couldn't see anybody around and all he could hear was the river. He would have to take his chances.

Taking a deep breath, he rolled on to his side, trying to stifle the low moan that escaped as a crippling pain shot through his body. Eventually he lay flat on his belly, panting heavily, sweat dripping from his brow. Then, gritting his teeth, he started to crawl towards the river.

Every movement was agony as he pulled himself across the stony river-bank. After what seemed hours he began to doubt he would make it as every fibre in his body begged him to stop and rest, but Dusty knew that if he stopped now he might not be able to start again.

Just then he noticed the river was louder and he could feel the dampness of the sand between the stones. It spurred him on and, before he knew it, his hands were splashing into cold, clear water. He plunged his head into the freezing shallows and drank deeply. The water was so cold it hurt his gullet, but he felt life flowing through him again.

He began to try and work out how long he been left for dead. It could've been minutes; it could have been hours.

He didn't know. But as he lay there he became aware of a new sensation coursing through his veins: anger.

Dusty was furious at being cut down like an animal and left for the vultures by Kid Cassidy and his henchmen. He was angry for all the poor suckers who would pour up to this part of the river and think they had struck it lucky, while all the while Craven and his crew mocked them.

Enough was enough! It was his turn to fight back. But he knew he needed help. If he could get back to Golden Gulch somehow, he knew he could persuade the miners to take back the town. He might even be able to find Jim before he left. His biggest problem was how to get back down the trail.

Slowly, he raised himself on to his arms, looking around to see if he could see Patsy. He gently whistled and called out her name. There was no reply. The mule would probably be long gone by now, frightened by the gunfire if the Kid and his men hadn't taken her.

He rested his head back on to the stones in despair. Golden Gulch was over a mile away and he could hardly stand, let alone walk. Although he couldn't see his wound, he knew he must be losing blood. Time was not on his side.

But Dusty was determined that this was not how it was going to end. He had to come up with something; and quick.

He lay listening to the river for a while, then looked up at it. The river was calm and shallow at the shore but Dusty knew that further out it would be deep and swift flowing. Wincing with pain, he managed to sit up and watch it pass for a while. A large long shadow which Dusty made out to be a log floated swiftly by, bobbing up and down on the silent, powerful current. He watched it travel downstream until it disappeared into the darkness.

And then it struck him. Golden Gulch was downstream! Eventually that log would pass near the town. That was the answer. The river would take him more quickly than riding a horse or mule — if he survived. He couldn't swim and he knew he wouldn't have the strength to keep himself afloat without something to hold on to. The more he thought about it, the more he convinced himself that the river was his only chance.

It was risky, but he knew for sure that if he didn't do something this was where he was going to die. He reckoned it was better drowning in the river trying to do something than just lying here and letting death take him.

With an almighty effort and a loud groan of pain Dusty raised himself to his feet and started to look up and down the shore for something that might possibly carry him down the river.

It didn't take him long to stumble across something that made him holler with delight.

The two nail-kegs that Craven's men had used to deposit gold in the river were lying discarded at the water's edge. He laughed out loud. The men who had tried to kill him might just have saved his life. With renewed vigour, he hobbled along to where the barrels lay and painfully bent over to inspect them more closely.

They were small enough to hold under each arm and he reckoned they would do the job of keeping him afloat. Both barrels had holes at the top and the plugs were nowhere in sight, which meant they would swiftly take in water making them useless. He started to rip the sleeves from his shirt, crying out with the pain of exertion. He stuffed the fabric into the holes, hammering them home with a rock to make them watertight.

Satisfied it was the best he could do, he rolled them to the river's edge where they gently bobbed in the shallow water. Dusty waded between them guiding them out to deeper water. It wasn't long before he was standing waist high and he gasped as the cold water took his breath away.

The two barrels weaved and bobbed like two live things wanting to be away, but Dusty held them tight, knowing that without them he would not survive for long.

He waded out a bit further, then felt his feet lift off the shale of the riverbed. The current began to turn him in slow circles but he was afloat, picking up speed and going in the right direction.

He just prayed that when the kegs arrived at Golden Gulch, he would still be holding on to them.

17

Jim felt he was drowning.

He was plunging through darkness, trying to get air into his lungs, but there was some great weight on his chest preventing him.

Then suddenly his eyes burst open and he managed to suck in a great lungful of air. His head felt as though it had split in two and his tongue felt swollen and dry but he kept breathing deeply as he looked around.

It was dark and gloomy, the only light coming from one feeble kerosene lamp. From what he could see he was in a tall wooden building with a couple of windows high enough to let light in but keep people out. He was sitting on a dirt floor. All around him were stacks of crates and barrels. When his breathing returned to normal, he tried to stand up and found his arms were tied behind him and that a rope was wrapped tightly around his chest and a post that went up to the roof. He pushed hard against the ropes but they didn't give an inch. He sat for some time trying to recall how he had got here and, more important, thinking how he was going to get out. He could just about remember leaving Edith's place and then . . . nothing. Everything after that was just a blank. He wondered whether she was OK.

He could just make out a door to his left; from behind it he could hear the raucous noise of a saloon, then it dawned on him where he was and who was behind his kidnap. This would be the store room of the Blood & Sweat. Then he heard voices and a key being turned in the lock.

In the gloom he couldn't make out the two men who came into the storeroom until one of them was almost standing over him.

'Ah, I see our guest is awake,' said Coleridge Craven, looking down at Jim with contempt. 'Enjoyed your little shut-eye?'

'What have you done with Edith?' spat Jim.

Craven's eyes narrowed. 'Don't you worry about Edith. She's no concern of yours. You've got a lot more to worry about.'

'Why's that?'

'Because tonight I get rid of you once and for all.'

'I didn't think even you would be low enough to kill an unarmed man.'

Craven smiled. 'Don't worry. You'll have a weapon. You know, since the hour you rode into Golden Gulch, you've been a real thorn in my side.'

'So why didn't you just get rid of me like you did with Jack Winsome?'

'Ah — you've been talking to Edith.'

Jim didn't reply.

Craven smiled. 'You could have been useful to me, but instead you went around poking your nose into things that don't concern you; but then again, I guess that's what a lawman is supposed to do.'

Jim looked up sharply.

'Oh, yes,' drawled Craven, 'we know who you are, Sheriff Jim Payne from Cedar Falls, Iowa.'

'Who told you?'

'He did.'

Craven turned to the side door where a figure emerged from the shadows.

'Michael!' cried Jim.

Craven started to pace the floor. 'I was thinking of getting rid of you the day you rode in but I'm glad I waited. No one misses a gold-digger, but this place would have been crawlin' with lawmen if a sheriff had disappeared.'

'They'll still come if I don't make it home.'

'True, but I'll be ready for 'em when they do. I got a saloonful of witnesses that you and your brother argued. Later you both got into a fight. You pulled a knife on Michael and he killed you in self-defence. I was a witness to it. Case closed.'

'Not even Michael's fool enough to

do your dirty work for you!'

'That shows how much you know your brother. Don't underestimate how much he hates you. He also has a pile of debts he tells me he's not gonna be able to settle any time soon. So we came to an agreement. I wipe his slate clean if he makes you go away.'

Jim laughed and looked up at Michael. 'Tell me you're not gettin' involved in this!'

Michael pulled a wide-bladed Bowie knife from the back of his belt and walked towards the pole that Jim was tied to. Suddenly he leaned behind his brother and with one stroke, sliced the ropes that bound his hands.

'Get up,' snarled Michael.

Jim sat rubbing the rope-burn circles around his wrists.

'I told you to get up!' said Michael and grabbed the front of Jim's shirt, dragging him roughly to his feet.

'This is it, little brother,' he said quietly. 'This is where we get to even a few scores. You've had this coming a long time. Ever since you let Pa die. Now you're my ticket out of here. Once I've dealt with you I can ride out of here and start again. I'll go back home and look after Ma until I come into my inheritance. I'll be set up nice. Looks like I struck gold after all.'

Jim stared into his brother's eyes.

'You're a fool, Michael! Always have been, always will be. You think this rattlesnake is gonna just let you walk out of here?'

'I'm tired of you tellin' me what I should do, little brother.'

'And to think I came all this way to try and talk some sense into you,' said Jim shaking his head in despair. 'I've wasted my breath, haven't I?'

Craven stepped forward. 'OK, break it up. That's enough of the family powwow. Let's get on with this.'

Michael took a few steps back into the centre of the dirt floor. He tossed the knife lightly from hand to hand, feeling its weight and balance.

Craven reached inside his jacket and

pulled out a throwing blade. He tossed it into the space between the two men, where it came to rest half-buried in the dirt.

'Pick it up, lawman!' ordered Craven.

'What if I don't? What if I'm not going to play your game?'

'Then your brother'll stick it to you anyway.'

Jim looked at each of the men in turn. 'You're crazy all of you! You've all been out here too long in this god-forsaken place. Put men together long enough where there's no law and order and you all end up behaving like savages!'

Craven watched Jim impassively. 'I told you when you first rode in here that I was the law. You didn't believe me then. Maybe you believe me now. Either you pick up that knife and fight like a man or you die like an animal. I don't care either way. It's up to you.'

The men's attention was distracted as the lock in the side door was opened from the outside and Kid Cassidy stepped into the storeroom.

'Well, well,' he said looking around him, 'looks like I nearly missed all the fun.'

'Where have you been?' snapped Craven.

'I was up at the new site supervising the boys.'

'Everything OK?'

'It is now. Had a spot of bother with the old digger who was pallying around with our friend here,' said the Kid, pointing at Jim, 'but he won't be giving us any more trouble.'

'OK,' said Craven. 'Let's get on with it.'

With a sinking heart, Jim knew there was only one way out of this. He had no choice. With a heavy sigh, he walked forward and lifted the knife.

Michael's eyes were wide and wild as he slowly walked towards his kid brother.

18

On the edge of town, where the tented city ended and the approach to the mountains began, Seamus Kilpatrick staggered out of the canvas saloon where he had been drinking since he had said his farewells.

At the time he had been genuinely sorry to see Dusty go, but in the mining camps where diggers came and went like luck, friendships were made and forgotten quickly. But still, Seamus had been fond of his old Irish pal.

As the cold night air hit him, he felt an urgent need to relieve himself of the gut-rot whiskey and watered-down beer he'd been pouring down his throat all night. He stumbled down to the riverbank, fumbling with the buttons on his canvas pants as he went.

At the water's edge he sighed as his strong stream splashed into the water.

Seamus let his head roll back and he stared up at the stars in the dark night sky, scattered like flecks of gold in the bottom of a pan. For a fleeting sentimental moment, Seamus wondered where his old pal was and would they ever see each other again.

'God bless ya, Dusty,' he muttered up to the night sky, 'wherever you are.'

The last drops splattered on to his scuffed boots and he buttoned himself up again.

He turned to make his way back to the saloon when he heard a noise in the dark, just loud enough to rise above the sound of the river. He stopped in his tracks, tilting his head, waiting to hear it again, but after a while he convinced himself it was nothing more than the wind.

He turned again, then stopped. This time he had definitely heard something like a low rasping wheeze.

Seamus didn't believe in ghosts, but if he had this would have been the noise he thought they would make. He took a deep breath and retraced his steps to the river, peering into the blackness.

'Hey! 'he called across the river. 'Anybody out there?'

He waited a minute before calling out again. 'Halloo! Anybody there?'

Nothing. He was starting to feel foolish, but just as he had decided it was the darkness and whiskey playing tricks on him, he heard it again. And this time, he was certain it was a man's voice.

'*Help . . . help me . . .* '

The voice was faint but unmistakable.

'Hold on, there. Hold on! I'm gonna get help!'

Seamus scrabbled up the riverbank back to the saloon. As he burst through the canvas flaps he shouted at the nearest group of men crowded round a makeshift faro table.

'You men! Grab some lights and follow me! Got a man out here in some kinda trouble.'

The men leapt to their feet and

followed Seamus with kerosene lamps and tar torches. Seamus led the troop to where he thought the voice had came from.

'Spread out, men. Spread out. Raise those lights high. There's somebody out there! I'm sure of it,' he ordered.

They did as they were instructed, spreading out in a thin line along the water's edge searching into the darkness. Then a cry went up.

'Over here! I got him!'

They gathered around the man who had raised the alarm. At his feet lay what looked like a pile of old rags. Then, with a low moan, the bundle moved. Seamus leaned over with a lamp.

'Holy Christ!' he cried, 'it's Dusty! Get back, boys, don't crowd him. Get blankets somebody! You go and see if you can find Ben Drummond, will ya? He did some army doctoring.'

As the men ran off, he knelt down beside Dusty and cradled his head.

'Dusty? Dusty? Can you hear me? It's

me, yer old pal, Seamus. Hang in there, pal.'

Dusty grabbed his old friend's hand and squeezed tightly. He tried to speak but all that came out was a low moan.

'Don't talk, Dusty. Save your strength.'

Seamus looked up at the crowd of men standing around them.

'For God's sake, ain't anybody found Ben yet? And don't just stand there — go get something we can use to carry him up to the saloon. We gotta get some heat into him. He's blue with cold! Gimme your jackets.'

Seamus stripped off his baggy coat and wrapped it tightly around Dusty's body. Another two or three men did the same.

'Go get something we can use as a stretcher.'

Seamus turned back to Dusty.

'Now you hang in there, old fella. Don't you go dyin' on me. Once we get you warm and cleaned up you can tell me who did this to you, all right? I'll make sure he was sorry he was ever born.'

Dusty tried to say something but the words would not form through his chattering teeth.

Two men returned from the saloon with an old table. They kicked the legs off and laid it beside the broken man. When they lifted him slowly on to it. Dusty let out a low, terrible groan.

'Easy, fellas, easy!' said Seamus. 'Now you four lads take a corner each and let's get him indoors. Hold those lanterns high.'

As they got him into the saloon Ben Drummond arrived.

'Make way men, make way!'

Ben removed his coat and hat and started to roll up his sleeves.

'Need lots of hot water and cloths I can clean this man up with,' he muttered looking Dusty up and down, 'And bring me some light. Can't see a damn thing!'

Dusty passed out again as Ben started to cut away his dirty shirt to reveal the deep bullet wound in his shoulder. Blood was flowing freely, soaking the makeshift operating table.

'Is it bad?' asked Seamus quietly.

'Seen a lot worse.'

'Is he gonna make it?'

'Bad shoulder wound. Lucky though, bullet's gone clean through. Lost a lot of blood. Put your thumb here.'

Ben felt Dusty's arms and chest with the back of his hand.

'He's freezing cold. Where's he been?'

'Fished him out the water. Don't know how long he'd been in there.'

'That's probably what saved him. Slowed his heart down. Would have bled to death on land.'

The barman arrived with a pan of hot water and a pile of rags. Ben soaked the rags and cleaned up the wound as best he could. One rinse of the cloth in the water turned it deep red.

'Any whiskey?'

Someone handed him a bottle. He took a quick mouthful, then splashed some over the wound to dissolve the congealed blood. Dusty let out a low painful moan. Seamus looked at Ben who smiled thinly.

'That's all right. If he's sore, he's alive.' He handed Seamus a length of cloth. 'Here, do something useful and tear this into strips for bandages.'

Ben took a tin plate from the bar and then poured in some gunpowder from a pouch on his belt. He took his gun out and, holding it by the barrel, started to pulverize the black grains into a fine dust. Taking one of the cloths, he scraped some lint from it with the edge of a knife, formed it into a little nest and then poured the gunpowder into the middle of it. He closed it over and put it over the wound.

'Gunpowder?' asked Seamus.

'Best styptic there is. Saved the life of many a soldier on the battlefield. Got those bandages?'

When Ben had finished off the dressing with a tight knot he wrapped a horse blanket around Dusty.

'Bank up the fire, keep him warm and keep him drinking liquids. He'll make it.'

Dusty's eyes flickered open.

'You OK, Dusty?' asked Seamus.

Dusty nodded and started to speak, but his mouth was dry.

'Here, have some of this.'

Seamus lifted his head off the table and poured a little whiskey over his dried and cracked lips. Dusty swallowed a little, then let out a rasping cough, spraying whiskey over his old friend.

'First time I ever saw you waste whiskey, Dusty. You must be sick. You still ain't told us who did this to you.'

'It was the Kid . . . and a couple of his boys.'

'Why'd they do it?'

'I caught 'em saltin' the river.'

'Where?'

''Bout a mile upstream . . . Jack Winsome was right . . . Craven has played us all along for suckers . . . for all this time . . . us old sourdoughs should have known better . . . '

Seamus stared into his old friend's eyes.

'And you came back to tell us?'

Dusty nodded. 'Had to. Gotta find Jim Payne. Gotta get him before Craven does . . . '

Dusty started coughing again and closed his eyes.

'OK. You take it easy.'

Standing up straight, Seamus addressed the room.

'Well? You heard the man. Let's find this Jim Payne; and then I think we got some scores to settle with Craven and his boys.'

Dusty grabbed Seamus's arm. 'Wait for me,' he said through gritted teeth.

'What? You're loco.'

'Came this far, you ain't stoppin' me now.'

Seamus laughed. 'OK, you old mule. Let's get you into a buckboard. The rest of you, get torches and guns. Spread the word. In one hour we meet outside the Blood & Sweat. Tonight, Golden Gulch belongs to us!'

19

In the storeroom the Payne brothers slowly circled each other, their knives glinting in the dim lamplight.

The Kid watched them with a smile of amusement. He leaned against the storeroom wall, his fingers tucked into his gunbelt, chewing nonchalantly on a piece of straw. Craven was more intent, his mean black eyes flashed in the gloom like an animal awaiting the killing of its prey.

The only noise was the tense, shallow breathing of the two men. Sweat dripped from their foreheads as each man waited for the other to make the first move.

Without warning Michael lunged forward with a loud grunt, stabbing at Jim's middle. Jim jumped back and stared into his brother's crazed eyes. There had been no risk of the knife causing harm but now he had all the proof he needed that his older brother was intent on going through with this madness.

He could hardly believe that Michael had once been the boy he had grown up with. Not just brothers but friends. He now knew that Michael was lost to him; a stranger he did not recognize.

Michael lunged again, shaking Jim from his thoughts. He stepped back, just missing the wildly slashing knife until he ran out of ground and his back slammed heavily against a wall. Michael's knife sliced through his shirt and he felt the sharp cut of flesh.

As Michael raised the blade to attack again, Jim lifted his foot and kicked him in the chest. Michael staggered back and Jim pushed off the wall and spun away.

'Stand and fight like a man, damn you! Don't make this harder for both of us!' shouted his brother. Spittle flecked across his lips.

'Wanna take a wager, Kid?' murmured Craven.

'Sure, what'd you think?' answered the Kid.

'Twenty bucks on Michael. I think he's got more to lose.'

'Don't know, Cole. I reckon the lawman's got your girl on his mind.'

Craven spun around and glared at the Kid.

'Make it forty!' he said grimly.

'Sure thing, boss,' said the Kid with a wide smile.

The two brothers were circling each other. Michael stabbed forward again but this time Jim was ready for him. At the very last second he twisted his body to the left just as the deadly blade flashed past his belly. Michael was leaning forward, his arm out full, all his weight on the front foot. Jim grabbed his wrist and, with a sharp twist, bent his arm up Michael's back. Michael howled in agony as he felt his elbow bend against the joint. Jim brought the horn heel of the knife down on the back of Michael's head with a sickening crack and Michael's legs crumpled. He fell to his knees and rolled on to his back. Jim knocked Michael's knife out of his limp hand and threw it across the storeroom floor, then he straddled him, pinning him with all his weight against his shoulders. He pressed his own knife against Michael's throat as his eyes flickered open.

'Why, you . . . !' Michael bucked his body and tried to roll Jim off his chest but Jim pressed the blade knife harder against Michael's throat.

'Steady now, Michael. Don't want to let this knife slip, do I?'

'I think you owe me forty bucks,' said the Kid in the corner.

Craven shook his head.

'No deal. It's not over until it's over. Finish the job, lawman,' he called.

Jim looked down at his brother and a deep wave of fury flushed through him. He despised him for allowing both of them to sink so low; for the deep betrayal of his family and everything his parents had brought them up to believe in.

'You would have killed me, wouldn't you, Michael? For a handful of gold. That's all my life was worth to you,' whispered Jim. He threw the knife away, balled his good hand into a fist and slammed it into Michael's jaw. Michael passed out as Jim struggled to his feet.

Craven approached the two men. 'I told you to finish him!' shouted Craven. 'Only one of you gets to walk away from this!'

'I ain't gonna do it, Craven. Not everyone in this town dances to your tune.'

'You think you're an honourable man, don't you? You think you're different, but I've met hundreds of men like you and I found their price. Everybody sells out in the end!'

Jim shook his head. 'I'm not for sale, Craven.'

'Then you're no good to nobody!'

Craven quickly reached down and

picked up the throwing knife Jim had discarded. Jim took a few steps away and backed into a stack of crates.

'There's nowhere for you to go,' said Craven as he slowly raised the knife above his shoulder. 'So long, Sheriff.' He took a deep breath and raised the knife the final few inches before it would spring from his hand. Then he paused. Outside, in the street, there was the sound of men shouting and hollering.

'What's that?' asked the Kid.

Craven was distracted for a mere moment, enough for his aim to be affected and as the knife spun through the air it started to falter. In the last split second, Jim moved his head to the left. He felt the draught as the blade just missed his cheek and stuck into the wooden crate with a dull thud, where it quivered like an arrow.

'Give me your gun, Kid,' shouted Craven, just as a window above his head shattered into a million pieces. A bottle with a burning rag in it sailed through the air and smashed on to the floor between Craven and Jim. Fire streaked across the floor in a pool of blue flames.

'Let's get out of here, Cole. We got trouble!' shouted the Kid.

'Give me your gun!' screamed Craven as smoke started to fill the storeroom.

Jim saw his chance in the confusion and threw himself between two large barrels.

'Leave him! Let's get outta here! The fire'll get him,' screamed the Kid.

The flames were now starting to catch on crates and bales of hay. The heat was becoming overpowering. Craven peered through the smoke, trying to find Jim but eventually gave up and followed the Kid out of the storeroom.

From behind the barrels Jim watched them go and heard the key turn in the lock. He ran across to the door and threw his full weight against it. It was solid. He ran across to the wall below the broken window.

'Hey!' he screamed at the top of his voice. 'Hey, can somebody get me outta here?' Outside, it sounded as though there was a full-scale battle. Amid the shouts and gunshots no one could hear him.

He ran back to the door. On a packing crate close to where he had been tied up, he saw his gunbelt. He unravelled it and belted it on.

Thick smoke was starting to fill the storeroom and he instinctively dropped closer to the floor where it was less dense. It was getting hard to breathe and not just because of the smoke. It was panic. He felt it constrict his throat and muddle his mind. Suddenly, he was ten again, back in the barn, with his father trapped below the plough. He had let his father die and now he was going to die the same way.

'Think,' he said angrily to himself. '*Think* . . . '

Flames were snaking up the walls towards the roof. He desperately searched around. There had to be something he could use to get out of this burning coffin, then his eyes alighted on the barrels he was hiding behind. They were labelled WHISKEY and they gave him an idea.

He knew it was a long shot but it was the best chance he had. If it didn't work, he would die here tonight.

20

When Edith caught the first whiff of burning timber she sensed something was terribly wrong. When the street filled with hoards of angry miners her forebodings were confirmed.

She'd seen trouble in Golden Gulch plenty of times before. Miners tearing up the town had become so much of a weekly ritual she'd almost got used to it. But tonight it was different. The men rioting outside were fuelled on something other than cheap booze and high spirits. They were angry and looking to vent their rage out on someone other than themselves. Edith felt sorry for whoever that someone was.

The other thing that was different was the burning. Of all the misfortunes that could befall a boomtown made of wood and canvas, fire was the one most dreaded. Edith had heard stories of places bigger than Golden Gulch being engulfed and consumed by fire in less than a day.

She stared out and cursed her luck. Another fifteen minutes and she would have been gone, but Golden Gulch seemed determined never to let her go.

She pushed Tommy back into the darkened café and let the carpetbags slip from her hands as she bolted the doors. She gave a moment's thought to the two horses that were saddled and waiting in the alley behind the café, but decided they would have to take care of themselves.

She pulled the blinds down on the windows and doors, hurried Tommy to the back of the café and made him crouch down behind the counter.

Edith ran through to the small living area and pulled open a wardrobe. She pulled aside the dresses she had left behind and pulled out a shotgun that had belonged to her husband. Considering it too large and unwieldy she had left it behind in favour of the handgun she had packed at the top of one of her bags. She rummaged in a drawer in her dressing-table until she found a box of ammunition. With a real effort she managed to break the barrel, shove two slugs into it and then snap it closed again before joining Tommy behind the counter.

'You OK?' she asked him in a whisper. She ran her hand through his hair almost to comfort herself as much as her son.

'I'm fine, Ma,' the boy lied.

Edith thought he looked white with worry in the dark and knew he was putting a brave face on it for her sake. She angrily asked herself why she hadn't left Golden Gulch before, when she'd had the chance. She swore to herself that if they saw tomorrow, that was exactly what she would do and nothing or nobody — not Craven, the Kid or someone like Jim Payne would stop her.

'What's happening out there, Ma?'

asked Tommy quietly, breaking into her thoughts.

'Don't know, son,' she answered truthfully and raised herself on her knees to look over the counter across the dark interior of the café, into the night. Main Street was filled with a mob of miners, many holding burning torches aloft. There were bursts of gunfire and the sound of breaking glass. For one of the few times in her life, Edith was racked with indecision. She just didn't know whether it was better to leave the café or stay where they were and try to sit out the storm. If she and Tommy put on old coats and hats, and if they were careful, she was sure they could slip out and mingle with the mob. But then what?

'D'you think he'll come and save us?' asked Tommy. His voice was quiet and small in the darkness and seemed to come from far away as though he was talking to himself as much as he was talking to Edith.

'I doubt it,' said his mother, 'I think

Cole Craven will have enough trouble on his hands tonight without concerning himself with us. Reckon he'll be holed up at the Blood & Sweat, same as us.'

'I wasn't talkin' 'bout Mr Craven.'

She looked down at his serious face in the darkness. 'Who were you referrin' to?'

'Why, Mr Payne, of course.'

Edith smiled and gave his shoulders a squeeze. Trust her boy to speak the hopes she had hardly dared think.

'I think Mr Payne will be far away from Golden Gulch. Least I hope he is, for his own sake . . . '

Whatever she was going to say was lost as the front windows shattered. She waited for a torch to come hurtling through or a group of men to kick in the door, but nothing happened.

'Stay here, Tommy and keep your head down.'

She stood up, gripping the gun tightly, and made her way to the front of the café, feeling anger instead of fear course through her veins. The first man that stepped foot through that door in her café and tried to hurt either her or Tommy would get both barrels in the guts.

She looked back over her shoulder to make sure Tommy was safe just as the front door flew open with a loud bang. She screamed, whirled round and raised the shotgun.

'For God's sake, Edith — put that damn thing down before someone gets hurt!'

Coleridge Craven and the Kid barged into the café. Edith felt a strange mixture of relief and disappointment at seing the two men.

'What's happening out there, Cole?'

Craven walked towards her and took the gun from her hands; his eyes were bright and wild. She had never seen him look this way before and she realized that for the first time since she had met this arrogant man, he was frightened.

Kid Cassidy stood beside the door,

looking out into the street nervously with his gun drawn. He was on edge, eager to be away.

Craven grabbed Edith's wrist and started dragging her towards the door.

'Let's get outta here,' he said as Edith pulled back with all her might.

'No! Stop! Cole — what is the matter with you? What's happening?'

'There's no time to explain. I'll tell you later. Come on!'

'Stop it!' screamed Edith as she struggled against his strength. 'Tell me now — what's got into you both?'

The Kid looked across from the door.

'It's over, Edith. We're through. They're on to us.'

'On to you? What does that mean?'

Craven stopped yanking at her and grabbed her forearms so roughly she let out a whimper of pain as he pulled her so near that his face was close to hers.

'They know. They know we were salting the river. One of 'em caught our boys doing it, red-handed. They thought they'd taken care of him but they didn't finish the job. Tonight, he turned up in town tellin' all these miners out there how we swindled them out of their cash. We had a good run, but it's over.'

'They're pulling the place apart looking for us,' said the Kid. 'They're gonna burn the whole place down with us in it if we don't get outta here!'

Cole looked deeply into Edith's eyes. 'But I ain't leaving without you, Edith. I want to marry you. We can start again, somewhere new?'

Edith couldn't quite comprehend what she had heard.

'You want us to . . . what? Are you crazy?'

'I'm tired of waiting for you, Edith but I ain't leaving you. We can leave tonight, but not before we get hitched.'

'You can't do this,' Edith almost screamed at him. 'You can't just demand that we get married. And then what? Do all this again? Run another scam until we're caught and get run out of town again?'

Craven stared at her grimly. 'It's your choice. You marry me tonight and we get you out of here or me and the Kid go now and you take your chances with a mob who might think you were in on it from the beginning.'

'You'd better choose and choose quick cos we ain't got much time,' the Kid called across.

Edith looked back to where Tommy was standing watching his mother. She saw the fear and disappointment in his eyes and she knew what she had to do. Her head fell. Any brief hope that Jim Payne might return now faded and died. Now marrying Craven seemed like a small price to pay to save her child.

'OK,' she said quietly, 'I'll do it.'

Cole smiled broadly and beamed at the Kid. 'That's my girl. See Kid? I told you she'd see sense. Let's go!'

Edith grabbed Craven's arm and looked intently into his eyes.

'But you gotta promise me something first, Cole . . . '

'C'mon . . . c'mon . . . ' said the Kid, looking anxiously out through the window as the noise of the crowd and the flames of burning buildings outside rose.

'Cole . . . promise me . . . '

'What is it?'

'You gotta promise me that no matter what happens, you'll look after Tommy. Promise me you won't let any harm come to him.'

Cole looked over at the boy standing over at the counter. 'I promise. Now let's go.'

They went out into the street, staying in the shadows of the buildings, and made their way to the Blood & Sweat. The Kid had pulled his neckerchief above his mouth to hide his face; Cole picked up an old miner's coat that had been discarded and threw it on.

Just as they were about to enter the saloon Cole stopped.

'What are you waiting for?' asked the

Kid. 'If we don't get off these streets we're gonna get lynched!'

'Him. Over there!'

The Kid and Edith followed his gaze.

In the middle of the street, the blind preacher was standing on his wooden crate in the middle of the street yelling at the top of voice, tears streaming down his face among the flames and destruction.

' *. . . for the great day of his wrath is come; and who shall be able to stand?*'

Cole turned to the Kid. 'Go get him.'

'What?'

'You heard me. Go get him.' He looked across at Edith. 'We need a preacher!'

21

Jim wrapped his arms around the barrel of whiskey and tried to move it. He realized how quickly he was losing strength as smoke filled his lungs.

He tried again and, with a loud grunt, he managed this time to tip it on to its edge. Then, as he gave a mighty heave, it fell over on to its side. He quickly rolled it towards the one wall that was not alight. The barrel banged against the wooden wall and came to rest. He turned to get another one. As he glanced around he saw his brother, lying still on the hay-covered floor. The worn soles of his boots were starting to smoulder as flames licked close.

Jim lifted him under his arms and dragged Michael between two stacks of crates.

'Michael! Michael! Can you hear me?' he yelled, patting him on his face.

176

But Michael did not stir. Jim put his ear to his chest. His heart was still beating.

Jim jumped up to get the second barrel he needed. It seemed to take for ever, but eventually the two barrels were side by side by the wall.

The temperature in the store was rising like the inside of an oven. His breathing was becoming shallower, and when he coughed his spittle was coloured black.

He gathered handfuls of hay, broken crates and anything else that might burn quickly around the two barrels. When he thought he had assembled enough, he looked for a place where he and Michael might be able to shelter from the worst of the heat. Almost every corner of the room was now ablaze, with flames streaking up the walls as though trying to find their way into the night air.

He found an old tarp and lay down beside Michael, covering them both with it as best he could to protect them from the burning embers drifting down from the roof. He wrapped a bandanna around his face, tied it tightly at the back of his head and took a long, deep breath before pulling out his Dragoon and taking careful aim at the right barrel. His first shot hit just below the ring of steel around its belly and the neat bullet hole immediately started to leak a stream of golden whiskey. It ran down the side of the barrel staining it black, then started to spread across the floor around the two barrels, where it burst into flames.

He watched the liquid for a minute or so; then, overcome by the heat, he lay back between the two stacks of boxes. All he could do now was wait, knowing that they didn't have much time.

He glanced across at Michael, who had not stirred, and found it hard to believe they might die together in a burning building. Just like their pa.

He lay back on the straw floor and, from a small pocket in the front of his belt, pulled out percussion caps and powder. He then carefully selected two .44 calibre ball shot, one for Michael and one for himself. He was no coward but he'd already watched a man burn to death. He didn't intend seeing two more. When the flames finally closed around them and he was sure his escape plan had failed, he knew what he would have to do to hasten their end.

A sound from the direction of the barrels made him sit up and look over. The whiskey-soaked debris around the barrel was well alight. Blue flames licked all around the barrels. Just a bit more time and those flames might just do their job.

He gazed up at the roof which was now fully alight. Edith came into his mind. He wondered where she was and hoped she was safe.

He suddenly felt tired and wanted to sleep but he shook his head fiercely. The thought of losing consciousness only to awake on fire was too frightening to think about. He shook his head from side to side, then his nose twitched. He could smell the warm vapour of boiling whiskey!

He sat up. The barrel he had holed was now fully alight and whiskey-flavoured steam was jetting out, rising up to the roof space. It was happening! The whiskey was starting to boil — but it was the sealed barrel that Jim had his hopes piled on. He stared at it intently and swore he could see, every now and again, small puffs of telltale steam escape from small gaps in the sides.

Above him, the roof began to creak and sag. A shower of sparks and embers came floating down upon him and Jim pulled the tarp around his head as small pieces of burning wood fell. All around him he could hear the sound of tortured planks protesting as they began to twist and warp in the heat.

Jim didn't know how much longer they could take it. Gripping his gun, he placed the end of the barrel against Michael's head. One small squeeze of the trigger and he would be delivered out of this fiery grave. Then he would turn the gun on himself.

He glanced again at the barrels. They were out of time. His idea hadn't worked and he had been crazy to ever think it would have. A beam fell from the roof and clattered to the ground, smashing crates and sending up a flurry of sparks and embers.

The crates around them were starting to scorch in the heat and flames were licking at the soles of his boots. He pulled his knees up close to his chin and noticed that the knuckles of his good hand clutching the tarp were beginning to blister.

For the first time since he had watched his pa die, Jim tasted bitter fear, like silver on the back of his tongue. It was time. He placed the barrel of the gun to his brother's head. The metal was hot.

'I'm sorry, Michael. This is the kindest thing I can do . . . '

He slowly started to squeeze the trigger and began to mutter a prayer under his breath.

That was when the store room exploded!

There was an ear-shattering bang and the wall gave way sending wood, smoke and flames out into the street. It was as though a tornado had swept through.

The barrels had gone and where they had been was now a gaping hole, through which startled miners were gawping.

Just as he'd hoped, under extreme pressure the heat had boiled the whiskey like water in the boiler of a locomotive and, with nowhere to go, the barrel had eventually exploded.

Jim dragged himself to his feet. The shock wave had extinguished some of the flames but the roof was still on fire and the noises from above reminded him that the roof could collapse at any moment.

With the last of his strength, he lifted Michael to his feet and hauled him through the breach in the wall until they both fell out into the muddy street.

The two men lay side by side, gulping fresh air. Nothing had ever tasted sweeter.

Michael stirred and started coughing uncontrollably. Jim reached over and patted his back.

'You OK, Michael?' he asked.

Michael's eyes flickered open and Jim let out a huge sigh of relief.

'You saved my life,' said Michael through racking coughs.

'Nothin' you wouldn't have done for me.'

'Would I? I tried to kill you.'

'But you didn't.' Jim smiled. 'Come on, let's get out of this mud.'

He hauled Michael to his feet and the two men made their way across the street to sit on the sidewalk. All around them was mayhem. The miners were rioting, firing guns and wrecking buildings. As they sat and watched, the Blood & Sweat's storeroom roof collapsed.

'I've been a fool, Jim,' said Michael quietly.

'Can't disagree.' Jim smiled.

'So where do we go from here?'

Jim looked at his brother. 'Now? I've got to find Edith and then I've got a score to settle with Craven. Then, if I'm still able, I'm going home.'

'OK then,' said Michael rising unsteadily to his feet. 'Sounds like a plan.'

'Where are you going?' asked Jim.

'I was thinking you might be needin' a little help. Least I can do.'

Jim smiled. 'I reckon I can use all the help I can get.'

'Well, what are we waitin' for?' said Michael and the two brothers made their way across the street to the Blood & Sweat saloon.

22

It was a strange wedding party that gathered in the office above the Blood & Sweat Saloon. Edith, Craven and the Kid lined up facing the blind preacher, who stood behind Cole's large desk as though it was an altar.

'Is everyone gathered?' he asked, raising his voice above the din in the street. From downstairs came the noise of breaking glass and smashing wood. The smell of burning wood was everywhere. The riot had moved from the street into the saloon.

'You got everybody you need, preacherman. Let's do this,' said Craven, who held firmly on to Edith's wrist and glanced at the Kid, who in turn looked anxiously at the door. He had posted Hank and Chuck outside in the corridor to make sure they weren't disturbed, but he didn't know how long they had.

'We could always do this later, Cole,' whispered the Kid, 'like somewhere a little quieter that ain't about to go up in smoke!'

'I've waited a long time for this moment, Kid,' said Craven, smiling down at Edith. 'We do it now.'

The preacher cleared his throat and began.

'Dearly beloved. We are gathered here today to witness the joining of this man and this woman in holy matrimony . . . '

The preacher started going through the wedding vows despite the sound of gunplay and fighting downstairs. As he spoke, the office windows got smashed but Craven told the preacher to ignore it and just keep going. They managed to get to the end of the ceremony in one piece.

'And so with the powers invested in me . . . ' began the preacher. Suddenly there was a loud banging on the door. Craven scowled at the Kid who drew his gun and ran across the room.

'Who is it?' called Hank.

'It's us.'

The Kid yanked the door. 'This had better be good,' he growled.

'You told us to come and get you if there was something you should know.'

'So c'mon,' the Kid snapped, 'what is it — we're kinda busy right now.'

Hank cleared his throat and brushed his hand through his hair. 'I don't know how to tell you this, Kid, but.'

'Spit it out, man!'

'It's the lawman. He's here.'

'That can't be,' said the Kid quietly. 'We left him for ash in the storeroom.'

'Well, he's downstairs now, with his brother, but he's comin' this way. He's askin' if anybody's seen Ms Winsome. He's lookin' for Mr Craven too.'

Craven and Edith looked across at the two men when they heard their names.

'What's the problem, Kid?'

'Payne. He's downstairs.'

Craven turned to look at Edith and

couldn't help notice that her eyes, dull and lifeless until now, suddenly sparked with hope at the mention of Payne's name.

'What d'you wanna do, Cole?' called the Kid from the door.

'Make sure he doesn't get up those stairs. I want him dead once and for all. Then get the horses ready. Once we're finished here, we'll meet you out the back and leave Golden Gulch to burn.'

'I'm gonna enjoy pluggin' this guy,' said the Kid as he headed towards the door.

' . . . and Kid?' called Craven.

'Yeah?'

'Don't you let him get away again. Hear me?'

'I hear you,' said the Kid, banging the door behind him.

Craven listened to his men go along the corridor to the top of the stairs before turning back to the preacher.

'Now, where were we?'

'I was just about to pronounce you man and wife.'

'Well, let's get on with it, then.'

'Have all the other men left the room?'

'Yeah. So what?'

'Then we can't proceed. There are no witnesses. We need witnesses before God.'

Edith couldn't help let out a small sigh of relief but Craven stared at the old man with fury. He walked beside his desk, pulled open the top drawer and lifted out a pistol. He cocked the hammer and placed the muzzle roughly against the old man's temple. The preacher flinched at the touch of cold steel.

'This is the only witness you need. Now you listen to me, preacherman. You get on and wed us or so help me, it'll be the last thing you do.'

'B-b-b-but you will not be properly married in the eyes of the Lord — '

'If you don't tell, I won't.' Craven grinned. 'If we ever get out of this hell-hole, it'll be our little secret. Now are you going to finish my wedding or am I going to have to organize your funeral. You choose.'

The preacher nervously cleared his throat. The Bible in his hands trembled.

'With the powers invested in me,' he croaked, 'I now pronounce you . . . '

His words were drowned out as the office door started to disintegrate into strips of wood beneath an onslaught of gunfire. The preacher sunk behind the desk as Craven grabbed Edith and hauled her behind the large settee. The gunfire raged for what seemed an eternity as Edith whimpered at every shot.

'They're giving that lawman and his double-crossing brother hell, ain't they?' murmured Craven. Then, almost as soon as he had uttered the words, the gunfire stopped as suddenly as it had started.

Craven waited a few moments; then he stood up and dragged Edith towards the desk. The preacher was lying curled in a ball on the floor. Craven kicked his foot and the preacher whimpered in fear.

'I got a gun pointing at your head. Say it.'

'I now pronounce you man and wife!' the preacher almost screamed.

Craven smiled. 'Do I get to kiss the bride?'

The preacher nodded his head vigorously from below the desk. Craven turned to Edith, grabbed her around her waist and kissed her roughly on her lips, but she didn't respond.

'Don't worry.' Cole smiled. 'We got lots of time to practise. I've waited a long time to do that. Let's go get the horses and get out of here.'

'Wait! We gotta go get Tommy,' wailed Edith.

'Too late for that now. We're outta here. He'll have to take care of himself.'

'No! You promised! You promised you'd take care of him. That's the only reason I agreed to marry you,' screamed Edith.

'You'll learn I promise lots of things, Mrs Craven. That don't always mean I do 'em. Now let's go!'

He pulled her roughly across the floor and hauled open the door. The hallway was filled with a thick pall of smoke.

Craven peered through the gloom and put a hand over his mouth.

'Kid? Kid? You there? C'mon, Kid, let's go!'

There was no reply.

'Kid? You there? You hear me?'

The smoke cleared a little and Craven stared down the corridor. Two bodies lay on the floor, each in a large, spreading pool of blood.

'See you got Payne and his bum brother,' called Craven. 'Is Hank and Chuck gettin' the horses? C'mon, Kid. Where are you?'

A draught of fresh air passed down the corridor and as the smoke cleared a little, Craven saw the Kid leaning against the wall near the top of the stairs.

'Hey, Kid, 'called Craven. 'Let's get outta here.'

The Kid looked up as though he had

seen Craven for the first time.

'They didn't make it, Cole,' he said quietly.

'Who didn't?'

Craven looked down at the bodies on the floor and recognized Hank and Chuck.

'They don't matter. As long as Payne is taken care of. Me and Edith, we're married now. Let's make tracks.'

A small smile spread across the Kid's face. 'Congratulations, Cole. Hope you'll both be . . . very . . . happy.' He started to sway, then fell forward and landed heavily face down in the hallway. The back of his shirt was soaked in blood. Edith let out a scream and Craven stared grimly at the Kid's lifeless body.

Then, through the smoke, two figures appeared at the head of the stairs at the end of the corridor.

'Congratulations, Craven,' said Michael.

'Sorry to spoil the honeymoon,' said Jim, standing shoulder to shoulder with his brother.

23

'That's far enough!' shouted Craven. He wrapped his arm around Edith's neck and pulled her close into his chest. He pressed his gun to the side of her head. 'You just don't know when to give up, do ya?'

'Let her go, Craven!' called Jim.

Craven shook his head and smiled widely. 'You don't get it all your own way, Payne. You got my partner, you got my town but you don't get the girl. No sir, this is one thing you don't get — the other thing you don't get is to walk away from here alive.'

Jim lowered his hand so it hovered over the handle of his Dragoon.

'Don't even think about it,' snarled Craven, 'I see that gun move an inch and she gets it. Now back up and get away from those stairs. Me and my wife are leaving town tonight.'

'What do we do now?' whispered Michael.

Jim looked into Edith's frightened eyes. He was sure Craven was bluffing. Normally he would have called that bluff, but this time it was different.

'We ain't gonna stop you, Craven,' he called.

'That's it.' Craven grinned. 'It's about time you started doing what you were told. You've been nothing but trouble since you arrived in my town. It's gonna give me great satisfaction getting rid of you.'

'You can go once you hand Edith over.'

'Don't you go trying to give me orders!' Craven screamed. 'I'm the one who gives the orders in Golden Gulch. Nobody else, hear me? I say what goes. Ain't that right, Edith?'

Edith nodded tearfully, her eyes wide with fear.

'I'm leaving and I'm taking my new wife with me and there's not a damn thing you can do to stop me!'

Craven suddenly swung the gun away from Edith and pointed it straight at Jim. With nothing to lose, Jim sprang forward towards Craven, trying to close the gap faster than Craven could adjust his aim. Edith pushed back against Craven, knocking him off balance, and the gun rose wildly into the air. And then Jim realized that Michael was by his side, having already thought the same thing. The two men thundered down the corridor charging towards Craven.

Craven wrestled with Edith. Then, seeing the two men approach, he swung the gun towards them. Jim watched in morbid fascination as Craven's finger slowly tightened on the trigger. And then he was being pushed roughly to the side as Michael thrust himself in front. Craven fired and Michael fell to the floor. As Jim ran forward, Edith grabbed Craven's wrist and bit into his arm as hard as she could. Craven cried out in pain and dropped his gun. He lashed out at Edith with the back of his hand; she fell heavily against the wall and slid down.

There was no time to stop. Jim jumped over his brother's body as it rolled on the floor and with the impetus carrying him forward, he leapt towards Craven, scrabbling with the gun to reload.

He hit Craven solidly in the ribs and both men fell to the floor. Jim was possessed with a fury he had never felt before. He dragged Craven to his feet by the lapels of his coat and turned him around. He swung at Craven's head. He felt his knuckles crack as they landed squarely on Craven's jaw. Craven stumbled back along the corridor towards the stairs but, before he could recover, Jim smashed his fist into his belly and felt a couple of ribs crack and give way. Craven roared with pain and continued to stumble backwards.

Jim raised his fist again, but before he could strike Craven fell heavily against the banister beside the stairs.

He shook his head to recover and put

both hands behind him on the banister to push himself back at Jim. As he did so, the wood cracked and splintered.

The banister sagged backwards and Craven fell on to the broken rungs, causing it to bend outwards even more. He stared at Jim venomously, then suddenly the whole banister gave way beneath his weight. With a final creaking and snapping, the woodwork collapsed and Craven fell into space.

He plunged through the smoky air, his arms and legs flailing to try and save himself. He crashed on top of the roulette table and let out an inhuman scream as the golden spike drove through his back and pierced his chest. He died with his eyes open, his blood seeping across the green baize table and scattered chips. Jim stared at him for a moment, then ran back along the corridor.

Edith was crouched beside Michael.

'Michael? Michael? Can you hear me?' said Jim, kneeling down beside him.

Michael's eyes opened and he smiled

when he recognized his brother.

'Did you get him?'

'I got him. Craven won't be troubling us no more.'

'Then I guess . . . I guess I don't owe him . . . any money.'

'You're square.' Jim smiled. 'Let's get you a doc.'

Michael shook his head and grabbed his brother's sleeve. 'No point in that, brother. I ain't got much time.'

'OK, take it easy.'

'Want you to do something for me . . .'

'Sure. Anything.'

'Tell Ma I'm sorry.'

'Sure, I'll tell her.'

'And . . . tell her, I saved you. I saved you, Jim, didn't I?'

Jim nodded. 'You saved my life, big brother.'

Michael nodded. 'I did something good after all . . .' A cough racked his body and he stiffened in pain as blood flecked his lips. Then he closed his eyes, his head fell to the side and Michael was gone.

24

Jim slowly stood up as Edith removed her shawl and spread it over Michael's face.

'I'm sorry, Jim,' she said and touched his arm.

'He was a good man. He just lost his way.'

The noise in the barroom downstairs grew louder and smoke was starting to fill the corridor again.

'We gotta get out of here. This whole place is gonna up like an inferno!' said Paynè, grabbing Edith by the wrist.

'Tommy,' cried Edith, 'we gotta find Tommy.'

'Where is he?'

'I left him at the Tuckered Out.'

'OK. Let's go!'

They made their way along the body-littered corridor, down the stairs and through the scene of mayhem in the saloon. Chairs, glasses and bottles flew through the air as Craven's men and the miners fought a pitched battle against each other.

The building was well alight and the flames had destroyed the fancy tapestries and scorched the paintings along the walls. Jim and Edith pushed their way through the mob and eventually made it into the night.

They looked around. Fire swept through most of the buildings on Main Street as though they were dried sagebrush. Golden Gulch was dying, burning slowly to death. Jim was not the sort of man who had ever taken the time to imagine what hell might look like. Now he had a good idea.

Horses reared, eyes white with fear and flanks flecked in sweat, as men wrestled to bring them to earth. Groups of miners ran everywhere almost in a blind panic. Some had made a half-hearted attempt at trying to form an orderly chain and were passing buckets of water from the river to the nearest building, but with little effect.

A few bottles of gut-rot had been saved and some men began dancing, whooping and hollering in the street like lunatics as the town burned down around them along with all their worldly goods.

'Are you OK?' asked Jim as they made their way through the bedlam.

'I'm fine,' replied Edith, gulping in great breaths of cool air.

Although the store next to it was ablaze, the Tuckered Out Café was almost untouched although, by the direction of the wind, Jim knew it was only a matter of time before it succumbed too. Edith pushed open the doors and ran into the dining room with Jim close behind. Smoke was starting to fill the room.

'Tommy! Tommy!' they both shouted.

At first, there was no reply, then they heard a small whimper; it came from behind the counter. Jim raced over and found Tommy curled up like a cat lying among the pots and pans. He lifted him up into his arms and headed towards the door just as flames started to come through the roof and one of the walls.

'Come on, Edith, let's get out of here!'

Thinking she was behind him, Jim ran out of the café and into the street. He placed Tommy beside a water trough, ripped his neckerchief from his neck and he dipped it into the water. Gently, he started to wipe the boy's head and face.

'He'll be fine, Edith, just got a little smoke in his lungs.'

When she didn't reply Jim turned, expecting to see her by his side. She wasn't there. He looked across at the café, which was now well alight. He saw through the smouldering curtains a figure moving across the room.

'Mom!' screamed Tommy. The boy jumped to his feet and would have run into the inferno if Jim had not grabbed him and held him close, gripping him to this chest. He felt Tommy's small body shudder and heave in his arms as small frightened sobs broke through his body, and he knew the boy was afraid that tonight he would become an orphan.

'What's happenin'?' cried a voice behind him. Jim turned and saw Dusty at the head of a crowd of men.

'You made it, son. Glad to see you,' said the old man. 'Come with us. Me and some of the boys are headin' down to the river. Reckon it'll be safer there. Fire's got a bit more to burn and things are going to get a whole lot crazier before the night is through.'

'Can't do,' said Jim, 'Edith's in the café.' Dusty looked at the building which was now fully alight with fire streaking across the shingles on the roof. Even as they looked, the windows cracked and shattered as the curtains lit behind them.

'Here. Hold the boy,' shouted Jim as he bundled the sobbing boy into Dusty's arms.

'Hell-fire, son. You ain't contemplain'tin' goin' in there, are you?'

Jim didn't reply. He looked around and his eyes lit on a horse trough — the same horse trough he had tossed Coleridge Craven's knife into on the first day he had arrived in Golden Gulch; it seemed a lifetime ago.

He picked up a blanket that lay discarded in the street. He then wrapped it around his head and shoulders and, to the amazement of the men looking on, put a hand on both sides of the wooden trough and lowered himself into the dark, cold water so that he was fully submerged. He rose again quickly, coughing and spluttering with the shock of the freezing water. He hoisted himself out of the crude bath and wrapped the blanket across his head and shoulders; then, without a backward glance or second thought, he ran across the street and into the burning building.

Even with the thick soaking blanket over him, he felt the punishing searing heat on his head and face. The smouldering floorboards cracked and warped with the heat, and he felt his feet scorch through his thick-soled boots. He raised his arm in front of him and started to call for Edith but the heat caught his throat, causing her name to die on his lips. He crouched low where the smoke seemed to be less but the heat was more intense.

And then he saw her. She was lying behind the counter, almost where they had found Tommy. Even as he made his way towards her the roof creaked and groaned as the main support started to warp and strain in the heat.

'Edith? Edith?' Jim called out as he made his way towards her. He knelt beside her, gently rolled her on to her side, almost afraid of what he might see. Miraculously, she had been untouched by the falling debris all around her, although her face was smudged black with smoke.

She clutched a battered old coffee pot with an ill-fitting lid. Jim tried to remove it from her grasp but could not prise her fingers from it. He almost laughed to think that this old piece of tin might cost them both their lives and for a moment, he wondered why she had risked her life to try and save it.

The roof complained loudly and Jim realized that there was no time to see whether she was alive or dead. He knew he might only have a few moments to save both of them and get out of this fire trap.

The heat sapped his strength and the smoke stole his breath. He looked up and could not see the door, but there was no time to define a clear path. He swung the blanket from his shoulders and covered Edith with it; then, with the last of his energy, he lifted her up. He ran, stumbled, fell towards the door. After only a half-dozen steps he felt his legs give way and knew he wasn't going to make it.

He let out a shout of defiance and gave one final push with everything he had left. They fell headlong out on to the wooden step. He felt his lungs fill with sweet fresh air, then realized that hands were grabbing him, taking Edith from his arms; then he was lying in the cold mud and slowly he felt the pain in his arms and legs subside.

He lay on his back sucking in large lungfuls of air in between bouts of coughing and watching the stars high up in the dark night sky. Then he heard Dusty's voice above his head.

'You all right, son?'

Jim nodded.

'That was a mighty brave thing you did there.'

Jim couldn't summon up enough breath to support words yet so he just nodded again. Then he raised himself on to one elbow, even though the effort of the movement made him cough and choke on the thick, black fluid that came up from his lungs.

'Edith . . . ' he managed to gasp, 'is she . . . ?'

But Dusty didn't reply. He was heading towards the group of men gathered around Edith, shouting at them to go and get Ben Drummond as fast as they could.

It was the last sound Jim heard before he passed out.

25

Jim stood in the cold, pale light of dawn and slowly surveyed what was left of Golden Gulch. The buildings had burned well into the night and now it was devastated; razed to the ground. There was hardly a plank of wood or stretch of canvas that had not been damaged by the fire. It had taken months for Golden Gulch to grow out of the sand and less than one day for it to disappear again.

Jim thought of other frontier towns that had suffered the same fate as Golden Gulch and had been rebuilt. They had risen, phoenix-like from the ashes, often better and stronger than before. But the difference was that those places had been built on a need for community and the desire to build a better place for everybody for generations to come. Golden Gulch had been built on pure greed.

The burning stench of destruction was everywhere and Jim knew that it would be weeks before he got the smell out of his hair and skin.

A few men were picking through the debris to see if there was anything to salvage but there was almost nothing; even picks and shovels had perished in the blaze. Hundreds of men had already left at first light either to go home or to move on to the next place where the rumours of gold, ripe for the picking, were already starting to circulate.

Seamus had organized grave-digging parties and was overseeing the grim task of burying what was left of those who had perished in the flames. Most were burned beyond recognition and were laid to rest in unmarked graves.

Rows of bodies yet to be buried were laid out with old tarps and blankets covering them. Jim surveyed the grisly rows, occasionally lifting the corners of the tarps to see if he could identify the person he now knew he loved. The blind preacher was walking among them, holding his Bible and saying a few words.

'... *ashes to ashes, dust to dust* ...'

He looked up and saw Tommy approach with two saddled horses.

'Hi, son. How are you this morning?'

'I'm OK, I guess,' the boy said quietly. 'A lotta people died last night, didn't they?'

'Too many,' said Jim. 'Been lookin' for my brother. Just don't seem right leaving without saying goodbye. I promised Ma I would bring him back. Even a body would be better than nothing.' He looked up and down the rows of bodies. 'All that diggin' and scrapin'. Most of 'em were only diggin' their own graves.'

'Mornin' Sheriff!'

Payne looked up and saw Dusty limping towards him.

'How you fairin', old timer?'

'Been better. Been worse.'

'How's the shoulder?'

'Ain't nothin' more'n a scratch.

Jim smiled at the old man's spirit then, glancing over at the boy to make sure he was out of earshot, asked the question he's been dreading.

'How's Edith?'

Dusty looked over Jim's shoulder.

'Why don't you ask her yourself?'

Jim spun round and couldn't believe his eyes. Edith was walking towards him. Her dress was tattered and burned around the hem and her hands and arms swathed in cloth bandages to the elbow. Her face was streaked with soot and loose strands of hair fell to her shoulders. But all Jim saw was her wide smile and sparkling eyes and he thought she was the most beautiful woman he had ever seen. He walked quickly to meet her and offered his arm for support which Edith gladly took.

'Edith,' he gasped. 'I thought . . . '

Edith smiled and blushed a little at Jim's concern.

'I know. I thought I was a goner too, but I'm fine considerin'.' She held out one of her arms. 'I ain't gonna lie.

These hurt like hell and they ain't gonna look pretty once I get these bandages off, but I was lucky. Dusty got me an old army doctor used to tending burns. Seems he covered them in cow-fat and took good care of me.'

'Don't thank me, miss,' beamed Dusty, 'if it weren't for the sheriff here, you'd be lyin' here among these others awaiting your turn to be dug in.'

'I know it, Dusty. I can't thank you enough for what you did last night, Mr Payne.'

Jim touched the edge of his Stetson and blushed. 'Don't mention it.'

'Are we ready to go, Mom?' asked Tommy.

'As ready as we'll ever be.'

'Where you headin?' asked Dusty.

'Not sure. Back to Montana maybe. We'll see.'

'You're travellin' light,' said Dusty surveying the horses.

'That's all we got left. Then again, I reckon it's about all we need,' said Edith as she put her arm around

Tommy's shoulders.

'Seems to me,' said Dusty, 'a young pretty woman and a boy shouldn't be trampin' cross country on their own. Anything could happen!' He stared pointedly at Jim. 'What d'ye think, Sheriff?'

'They should be all right if they keep to the main trails,' Jim said.

Dusty took off his battered hat and slapped it against his thigh in frustration. 'Dammit boy! For a bright man you sure are thick as a fence post sometimes.' He turned to Edith. 'And as for you, young lady, you're just as stubborn. Why don't one of you say what needs to be said!'

Edith and Jim looked uncomfortably at each other. Then Jim cleared his throat.

'Miss Winsome, I'm leaving town too and it would be no problem if we travelled along together for a while. It's a mighty long way for a man to travel with nothing else but his thoughts to keep him company. And if you've got no particular place to go you could come back to our place. You could meet Ma and rest up for a while then decide what your next step is gonna be.'

'That is a very considerate proposition, Mr Payne,' said Edith with a smile. 'I'd like to take you up on your kind offer.'

'That OK with you, Tommy?'

'Yessir! Fine by me!' Tommy beamed.

'Awright! That's sorted then!' shouted Dusty. 'Now git on your way afore one of you changes your mind!'

'Where will you go to, Mr Murphy?' asked Tommy.

'Oh, don't worry about me, sonny. I'll go where the winds take me just like I've always done. Now, I don't like long goodbyes, so if you don't mind I'm gonna finish up here and be on my way. Good luck to y'all.'

He ruffled Tommy's hair, blushed when Edith kissed him tenderly on his cheek. He grasped Jim's hand and shook it warmly.

'Goodbye, Jim. Look after them.

Seems to me you're the only one leavin' this god-forsaken place with anything worthwhile.'

'Thanks for everything, Dusty,' smiled Jim.

' 'Tweren't nothin', said Dusty. He pulled a large red neckerchief out of his pants and blew his nose loudly. Then, without a backward glance, he walked away.

'Ready to go?' asked Jim.

Edith looked over and saw the preacher wandering among the corpses.

'Hold on. There's something I gotta know before I leave.'

She walked over to the old man and touched his sleeve. He looked up with unseeing eyes.

'Excuse me, preacher. You remember me from last night?'

'Yes. Yes I do. The marriage ceremony.'

'That's right. I wanted to ask you something.'

'Sure, sure.'

'The thing I wanted to know. Am I

. . . I mean, was I properly married to Cole Craven last night?'

The preacher shook his head.

'There has to be witnesses. There weren't no witnesses. Ain't legal without witnesses.'

'There were witnesses for most of it. It was only at the end.'

The preacher looked perplexed.

'Was there? I didn't see nobody and if I didn't see nobody, it weren't legal.'

Edith smiled widely and brushed the old man's arm.

'Thank you, preacher.'

She walked back over to the horses. 'Guess we're ready to go,' she called.

Tommy jumped lightly into his saddle and Jim walked over to help Edith into hers.

'Do you mind if I ask you something?'

'Sure,' she said.

'What was so important about that old coffee pot that was worth nearly getting killed for? I had to prise it out your hands.'

'I'll show you.'

She unbuckled the saddle-bag and gently lifted out the battered coffee pot. Jim watched her curiously as she pulled off the lid and slipped her thin hand into it, pulling out a small canvas bag which she pulled apart.

'Hold out your hand, 'she said.

Edith tilted the bag towards the palm of his hand. A small rivulet of golden sand poured out, making a small pile in Jim's palm.

'Most of my customers didn't have cash so they paid me in gold. I got enough here to set me and Tommy up for the rest of our days. I kept this stashed in an old coffee pot thinkin' nobody would ever look for it there. That's why I had to go back for it.'

Jim laughed as he carefully let the gold dust slide from his hand and back into the bag. When the coffee pot was back in the saddle-bag, he helped her into the saddle.

'Let's get outta here,' called Jim as he swung into the saddle of his grey roan.

The three of them spurred their horses forward. As they rode into the morning, Jim couldn't help but notice Edith's long, blonde hair flash in the sunlight.

It was like strands of pure gold.

THE END

We do hope that you have enjoyed reading this large print book.

Did you know that all of our titles are available for purchase?

We publish a wide range of high quality large print books including:
Romances, Mysteries, Classics
General Fiction
Non Fiction and Westerns

Special interest titles available in large print are:
The Little Oxford Dictionary
Music Book, Song Book
Hymn Book, Service Book

Also available from us courtesy of Oxford University Press:
Young Readers' Dictionary
(large print edition)
Young Readers' Thesaurus
(large print edition)

For further information or a free brochure, please contact us at:
Ulverscroft Large Print Books Ltd.,
The Green, Bradgate Road, Anstey,
Leicester, LE7 7FU, England.
Tel: (00 44) 0116 236 4325
Fax: (00 44) 0116 234 0205

JAKE RAINS

Tony Masero

Cuba, 1898. When Jake Rains' best friend and fellow Rough Rider was fatally wounded, he promised to care for his widow — though Kitty Cartright's protector is Chris Leeward, owner of the L double E ranch. Jake arrives in Oakum and things look bad. There's trouble at the Cartright place, so Jake and his new friend, Sam, are determined to put things right. But as they face Leeward's band of vengeful mountain men, Jake must fight for his life.

A MAN CALLED BREED

Chuck Tyrell

They call him Breed . . . and when he is threatened with violence — because of his Indian heritage — he severely wounds Reed Fowley and seeks refuge in the desert. But Fowley, with his father and brothers, makes sure he's found — locating his homestead in Lone Pine Canyon, below the Mogollon Rim. They hire Robert Candless and a band of savage outlaws to kill him. Now, Breed and Blessing, his wife-to-be, along with his protégé Sparrow, must fight for their lives . . . or die.

IN THE HIGH BITTERROOTS

Will DuRey

They rode out as the snow began to fall. The seven men were to rescue a band of travellers trapped by an avalanche in the high Bitterroot Mountains. But once clear of the Montana township of Wicker, it's apparent that the on-coming winter blizzards are not the only threat to success. The swiftly assembled group members bring their own grievances and evil. Moreover, the mountain holds an unexpected threat for young Jess Clarke, and 'Doc' Hames.